"Great combination of police work and just a hint of the supernatural. Eagle Feather always brings it for his Native Americans as well. Right, White Man? Ha...good story, good friends."
Amazon Reviewer

"A too-long awaited Book 7 in the Zack Tolliver Mystery series by R Lawson Gamble, Las Cruces is, as always, an outstanding addition to any Western adventure thriller fan, that's sure to win a new multitude of fans for Zack, Eagle Feather and their creator."
Rosemary Kenny

LAS CRUCES

A Novel

Zack Tolliver, FBI Series Book Seven

R LAWSON GAMBLE

To Zack fans worldwide who by reading keep me writing,
and to Cort for just being Cort!

Special thanks to Super Reader Craig for his usual enthusiastic and perceptive critique and especially for his engineering knowledge of gas and oil pipelines!

PREFACE
1864

It was happening again. She felt the old familiar dread clutch at her gut and throat, the horror she had somehow reduced to background noise over the months and years, those nights of sitting bolt upright in her bed with her heart beating a tattoo so that it must burst from her chest, the images of blood and the sound of the gunshot and the whine of the bullet vivid in her nightmare, those desperate moments relived but mercifully obscured and faded by the veil of time.

It was happening all over again. They were here again. They were killing George with their knives and now turning their bloodlust upon her. Once again the window loomed as her only escape, a square frame into the black unknown. Once again she thrust, scrambled, threw herself over and through it, onto the hard ground, rolling, gasping, her hoop-buoyed skirt snagging. She found her feet, ran down the slope toward the creek, toward the road, seeking help. But this time her toe caught, she pitched forward screaming, fell and before she could rise again rough hands grasped and held her. She fought with all the fury born of terror until a stunning blow to her head turned her senses dull. She felt herself dragged on her stomach by her feet up the hill, her hoops snagging, encircling her upper torso like a cage. She tried to help herself, grasping at roots, grass, the hard dirt, her nails tearing, bleeding. But they were too strong for her.

It was happening all over again, and this time she would not escape.

CHAPTER ONE

Zack Tolliver sat back in the ancient wooden swivel chair, his arms folded across his chest, long legs stretched out and crossed under the desk, unseeing blue eyes on the upper corner of the window where the early morning sun ignited frost crystals into a thousand sparkling diamonds. The aroma of coffee and sausage hung comfortably about him, the faint chatter of Libby and little Bernie at play in the den came in snatches. A part of Zack's mind was comforted by these loved manifestations of home and family, but his immediate focus was upon the official Federal Bureau of Investigation communication on the computer screen in front of him—enigmatic, intriguing. He read it once again.

To: Deputy Assistant Director Zack Tolliver, Director of Special Cases
From: Special Agent James McLeish
Re: CCRSB Criminal Case 1845-F
Sir;
I was advised by Executive Assistant Director Bradford to consult you regarding the above case. I was unaware of the Special Cases Unit, as apparently it is new to the branch, and could find no structure or protocol for it. I am not clear what constitutes a "special case." Hopefully, this one falls within your purview. The situation is extremely sensitive and involves inexplicable events of such a nature I feel it necessary to present it in person. Time is of the essence. I can fly to Flagstaff to meet you whenever it is convenient for you.
Sincerely,
James McLeish

A moment later, the phone rang. Zack glanced at it, picked it up.

"Good morning, Zack. How are you?"

Zack recognized the smooth, sensual, yet efficient voice of Supervisory Agent Janice Hooper. He could almost hear her smiling.

"Good morning, Janice. I am well, thank you, and I'm going to assume your call and the memo I just received on my computer screen are related in some way."

"It wasn't Director Bradford."

Zack was momentarily confused, a not unusual circumstance when speaking to Janice. "What wasn't?"

"It wasn't his idea to send McLeish your way. It was mine."

"Oh. Why?"

"Two reasons. First, it's about time we get your unit rolling. Once you've got some work under your belt, and some successes, agents will send more cases your way." She paused. "Second, this case may have some interesting elements."

"What's it about?"

"Go find out. Make an appointment with Special Agent McLeish. You should hear it from him first." She hung up.

Zack resumed staring out the window. His retirement from the FBI must have been the shortest on record, he thought. It had begun just months before when he realized the time he spent on the road working those cases that seemed to require his particular talents or on the lecture circuit speaking about them meant he wasn't able to be a husband to his wife Libby or a father to his little boy Bernie. Libby had verbalized the same thought to him, quite clearly. He had retired.

It was not to be. When Libby's sister's family came under threat from a killer, the local police were ineffectual and the FBI lacked jurisdiction. Zack took action. Using his old FBI contacts for information and aided by his friend and former mentor Eagle Feather, he worked informally with the local sheriff's office. When the FBI was finally drawn into the case, he served as a liaison between the sheriff's office and Special Agent Janice Hooper. The case was solved, but not before Zack had a very uncomfortable moment in a dark cave with an unidentified creature.

Zack's ear caught a random snatch of song from Bernie. He smiled. The upshot of it all had been the offer of a new job with the FBI, an Assistant Directorship as Head of a brand new unit in the FBI Criminal, Cyber, Response, and Services Branch named the Special Cases Unit, meaning those cases too sensitive for other agents to handle, culturally or spiritually. Or, as Eagle Feather had dubbed it, the Ghost Unit. Janice Hooper had engineered its creation, Zack had no doubt. The big carrot? He could work from home. And he could turn down those cases he deemed too mundane or unsuited to his special skillset. Best of all, Libby was all for it.

There had been some calls. He had turned them all down. Agents were struggling to understand the purpose of his unit, mistaking it for a depository for those cases they'd rather not take on. He hoped this new case did not turn out to be one of those. Still, this was the first time Special Agent Hooper, his nominal boss, had intervened. So, of course, he would drive to Flagstaff to meet Special Agent McLeish. At worst, if he declined this case as well, he could run some errands in the city he'd been putting off the last few weeks.

His reply message to Agent McLeish was answered immediately with a phone call, and he and McLeish agreed to meet in Flagstaff that afternoon at two p.m. Zack suggested the FBI Office conference room, but McLeish demurred.

"I'd rather we meet a little less formally," he said. "Do you know the Downtown Diner? The coffee sucks, but the food is cheap and no one important ever goes there."

Zack was intrigued by McLeish's words. He felt his curiosity about the case grow. He extricated his legs from under the desk and ambled over to the day room where Libby and Bernie were working on a large intricate puzzle on the carpeted floor.

"Hi, Daddy," Bernie said without looking up, his eyes searching the unused puzzle pieces.

"I heard the phone ring twice," Libby said. Her brown eyes held the question. "Busy morning."

Zack grinned. Libby lay on her stomach, her ankles crossed, her chin on her elbows. Bernie sat cross-legged opposite her, the puzzle between them. They were in perfect synchronicity. Zack etched the picture in his mind.

"Another case referral," he said. "This one might even work out."

Libby leaned onto her side to look up at him. "Are you leaving?"

"Not until after lunch," Zack said. "I'm meeting an agent in Flagstaff." He leaned down to pick a puzzle piece from the rug. "Doesn't this—?"

Bernie rolled an eye at him. "Don't help, Daddy."

Zack put both palms up. "Okay, okay. I won't help."

Later, driving south on Rt. 89 toward Flagstaff, he thought about that moment and chuckled. His job description was ideal, no doubt about that. Chances were this case wouldn't meet his qualifications either, and he could run his errands and head right back to home and hearth. But another part of him hoped that would not be the case. He felt a certain restlessness, a need to be active.

The Downtown Diner proved to be a glass-front hole in the wall on a busy city street. It was certainly innocuous enough. As he pulled open the heavy glass door it occurred to him he had no way to identify Agent McLeish. That concern evaporated immediately. There was only one person in the place. He was sitting at a table halfway along the mirrored wall of the diner. Zack walked toward him.

"Agent McLeish?"

The man had been watching him approach. He had an abundance of sandy hair and deep smile creases carved into his cheeks, which grew as Zack approached. He was a big man, looked to be in his mid-sixties. He half stood, put out his hand.

"Agent Tolliver. Thank you for agreeing to meet me."

Zack shook his hand, nodded. "I had a little push from Janice Hooper. She seems to think you have something interesting to say."

"I do. The question is, what will you think of it?" He had a dish of pastry in front of him. "As I said, the coffee sucks but the strudel is delicious."

Zack caught the eye of the waitress and pointed at McLeish's strudel. His attention went back to McLeish. "So?"

McLeish had taken a bite. He chewed it slowly, thinking. Then he twirled his fork toward Zack. "First, some background. I'm out of the LA office, but I live in Santa Barbara. Most of my cases come from there." He leveled blue eyes on Zack. "Are you familiar with the area?"

"Somewhat."

"I'll try not to bore you with what you already know. The city of Santa Barbara rests on a coastal shelf between the Pacific and the Santa Ynez Mountains. This coastal shelf begins just north of Ventura and swings west hemmed in by the mountains up through Summerland, Montecito, Santa Barbara, and Goleta until it narrows and finally disappears altogether at Gaviota, where the mountains meet the sea. At Gaviota, a huge fault or uplift allows access to the interior along a stream bed. Before the highway was carved and tunneled through it, the gorge was so narrow it was difficult for two men on horseback to pass one another. Once through the gorge, you come to a region of soft foothills. Here the road divides, one branch heading northwest toward Lompoc, the other northeast toward Buellton and the Santa Ynez River Valley."

"I've seen the area," Zack said. "It's beautiful."

"It's beautiful, all right, but it's rough. Back in the day, it was a great place for bandits and a natural habitat for bear and mountain lions. From the beginning of our knowledge, the place attracted all sorts of predators, including human."

Zack eyed McLeish over a forkful of strudel. "I'm guessing even today?"

McLeish pondered that. "Well, yes...and no. I can answer you best by telling the story."

Zack nodded for him to continue.

"More background. Again, apologies for rehashing old news. All the way back in Spanish times, the Spanish Crown began rewarding deserving citizens with grants of land in Alta California. After Mexico won its independence, the new leaders continued the practice. Soon the entire coastal shelf I just described had been claimed and much of the area north of the Gaviota Gap. The land I described earlier just beyond the gorge where the roads divide was granted to a retired Spanish soldier named Cordero. It was called Las Cruces, Spanish for The Crosses. Legend says the name came from crosses the Franciscans erected over Indian graves at an old Indian battle site. No one today seems to know exactly where they are." McLeish paused. "Those were the first recorded killings we know of at that place, but would not be the last."

"Weren't Chumash battles uncommon? I thought they were rather peaceful people."

McLeish nodded. "Well, yes, they were, which is what makes this place all the more, uh, shall we say, interesting." He paused to sip coffee. "Anyway, the Gaviota gap has always been one of three semi-reasonable approaches to the Santa Ynez River Valley that lies north of the Santa Ynez Mountains from Santa Barbara. If you wanted to reach La Purisima Mission without taking the time to ramble all the way around Point Conception, you went through the gap. If you wanted to get to Santa Ynez Mission without climbing over a pass, you also braved the gorge. For most, it was a bit of a harrowing experience. An old-timer told me his grandparents would take two days to get to the gorge from Santa Barbara by wagon, then they would have to send someone ahead to the Las Cruces Adobe at the road divide to fetch a few Indians to help tilt and lift the wagon through the passage; it was that narrow."

"Great place for an outlaw gang," Zack said.

"Oh, yes. So, over the years the reputation of the place grew, and not in a good way. The Las Cruces Adobe spent a fair amount of its existence as a den of whores, card sharks, or anything a saddle tramp might enjoy. The Santa Barbaraños tried to ambush Fremont and his American army there, but he went another way. There have been robberies and shootings and killings of every description right up to modern times." He paused. "And now I guess we can add modern times as well."

"So someone's been killed there."

"We think so."

Zack's eyebrows went up. "You *think* so?"

McLeish gave a mild grin, shrugged. "Got to get back to my story to explain. About 1860 or so, the stage line was looking for a stage stop north of the gorge where the road forked to go east to Santa Ynez or west to Purisima Mission and Lompoc and on up the coast to San Luis Obispo. Three brothers named Williams were living in the Las Cruces Adobe and added a barn and put in a bid for the stage station. It would mean a lot of money to those folks at that time. Then along comes a couple named Corliss who built a home near there and put in their own bid. Well, things got fractious. According to testimony, one of the Williams brothers even tried to bribe the dairy girl to poison the Corliss' milk, but she wouldn't do it. The Corliss couple got the bid.

"Well, not long after that the daily stagecoach discovered the Corliss' bodies in the burnt out hulk of their home. Their bodies were laid in an X pattern in front of the fireplace, the husband face down, the wife's body on top of him, the scorched metal hoops of her dress up around her neck. The investigating posse figured she had been dragged into the building by her feet—I guess they even found fingernail marks in the dirt to show she was still alive at the time."

"Good god!"

"Yeah, pretty gruesome. At first, they thought the hired hand had done it, but later they found him wedged between a couple of boulders, his body mutilated, throat cut, partially scalped."

"The Williams brothers?"

"Yeah, the responding sheriff's posse from Santa Barbara figured it had to be them, there were no other solid suspects. There was a trial, but with no real evidence, there was no conviction. The murders were never solved."

Zack raised an eyebrow. "Well, thanks for the interesting story and the history lesson. I enjoyed it, and I enjoyed the breakfast. But why am I here?"

McLeish paused, took another sip of coffee, and grimaced. When he put it down, there was no trace of humor in his expression. "All that happened in 1864, over one hundred fifty years ago. That whole area is a state park now. Two days ago, a hiker wandered off the trail and stumbled over a body. It was a woman's body, although it was hard to tell because she'd been pretty badly burnt."

"The body was burnt?"

"That's right. And get this. They had trouble examining the remains because some sort of metal bands were fused together over her neck and face." McLeish was watching Zack closely.

"You mean like...?"

"Yeah, like hoops for a dress from the mid-1850s. And that's not all. I did a little digging around and a little research. There is no doubt in my mind the woman's burnt body was left on the exact spot where the Corliss cabin had once stood."

CHAPTER TWO

Zack kept his gaze on McLeish. "Who is the woman?"

"We don't know yet. The fire was hot, an accelerant was used. Hands and feet are basically bone, no help there. The metal from the hoops fused with her face, which was burnt beyond recognition anyway. No teeth. She may have worn dentures, but they haven't found them. All we know is she was not young. No one has reported any missing females."

"DNA, compare it with Corliss family descendants?"

McLeish nodded. "Yeah, that's the only possibility we can come up with. It's in the works if we can find a family member. The surname Corliss is popular, even around there, but we haven't found a close link. We're working outward geographically from Central California, but no luck yet."

"Age, height, former injuries, anything like that?"

"Forensics puts her age between fifty and eighty, not much help. They've got too little to work with. The forensics people say her bones appear uninjured. She has no deformities or other distinguishing characteristics. They put her height somewhere around five foot five inches." McLeish frowned. "That narrows it down, right?"

"Well, you've got a tough one, all right. I'm sure you are checking the accelerant used, looking for prints and other signs at the scene, asking who saw what when." Zack shrugged. "Not much else you can do. But again, why me? Despite the historic angle you've described, all you have is a difficult case and a lot of work in front of you. So why come to me?"

McLeish looked down into his empty coffee cup, paused, and mumbled, "The ghost."

"The ghost," Zack repeated, staring at McLeish.

The agent gave a somewhat embarrassed grin. "The ghost is why I called you in."

Zack sat back, crossed his arms. "I don't do ghosts."

"You have before."

"Look, I'm not a necromancer, spiritualist, ghost hunter, fortune teller, or the like. I'm a realist. I look behind the facade and find the real reason for the display."

"That's all I'm asking. Help me find the real reason for the display."

Zack sighed. "Okay, tell me about the ghost." He grimaced. "No promises, though."

"Fair enough." McLeish sat back. "I told you it was a wayward hiker who found the body. The Gaviota State Park is a huge place, chock full of hiking trails that follow original roads and paths used since ancient times by the Chumash Indians. This particular path is called the Ortega Trail. It roughly follows the original road from the Las Cruces Adobe down into the gorge along the stream. Imagine abrupt rising hills on both sides slashed by deep, dark ravines choked with old growth and hundred-year-old oak trees with foot-thick branches that reach out here and there like massive arms ending in long, spiny fingernails. Nearer the gorge, the hills are split open becoming perpendicular rock walls." McLeish noticed Zack's expression. "This may sound like hyperbole, but I tell you, man, it's a place out of nightmares, especially at night."

Zack started to speak, but McLeish put up a palm. "Let me finish, then you can make all the cracks you want. The original Corliss place was built upon a grassy plateau between two ravines. It's a prominent spot. The cabin, or Adobe or whatever it was would have been visible as soon as the traveler emerged from the depth of the gorge, probably a welcome sight back then. Today, the Route 101 northbound lanes emerge from a tunnel and round an ascending curve that points the driver right at this knoll. During the day, with the building long gone, you just see a blend of rock and vegetation on the side of a steep hill, nothing special. At night, of course, you see nothing at all. There are no lights in the gorge other than passing vehicle headlights and the lights within the tunnel.

"About two weeks before the body was found, the highway patrol started getting weird reports from car travelers describing a figure they saw at night on the hillside in front of them as they emerged from the tunnel and came up around the curve. The figure appeared to dance, kind of hopping around and throwing up its legs one after the other."

"How could they see it, in the dark and all? Did their headlights illuminate it?"

McLeish laughed. "Oh, no, no, no. That would be far too easy. They could see the figure because it was on fire."

Zack felt a strange reaction in his gut. "Okay, so what did the CHP do?"

McLeish gave a slow shake of his head. "After the first report or two, they promised to take a look. The fire department checked the area but found nothing. The CHP has units traveling that stretch of road fairly regularly, and given the wine tasting draw of the valleys beyond, the cops are alert for about anything—other than flaming figures dancing, I guess. But when more reports came in, almost on a nightly basis, they ran units through there more frequently. None of the cops ever saw a thing. So they put it down as a joke, or local myth, like the girl hitchhiker who has the driver deliver her to the local cemetery—you know that one?"

Zack grinned, nodded.

"So they laughed it off, at least until the hiker stumbled onto the burned body."

"You think this killer is trying to capitalize on the history of the place for some reason. At least, I assume that's why you gave me the history."

"I do."

"You think the old murders and the cabin burning may go to motive in some way?"

McLeish shrugged. "It's all we've got."

Zack's chin dropped to his chest in thought. "The people who saw the figure on fire, she was always dancing?"

"Yeah."

"No shadows, no other lights or movement to indicate another person was there?"

"According to the motorist reports, no. Obviously, someone had to have been there, but no one saw any indication of it. We found no sign later, either."

"How much have you learned beyond the history you have already given me?"

McLeish grinned, reached down next to his chair and extracted a paper file from his briefcase. He flipped it on the table so it skidded toward Zack.

"It's all there—history as far as we've been able to learn it, including neighbors and likely travelers at that time, forensics report, investigators' reports, reports from the travelers who witnessed the fire dancer, all of it. You coming aboard?"

Zack had already made up his mind. He stood, extended a hand to McLeish. "Yeah, my team will give you a hand. I'll be out there first thing in the morning. Is Vandenberg Air Force Base anywhere near there?"

McLeish stood. He was even bigger than Zack had first thought. "Yep. Just fifteen miles or so."

"Great. I can get a ride into there, maybe borrow some wheels at the base. Got some connections there."

"I thought you had a unit, a team?"

Zack grinned. "Yeah, my team will come out when he's ready. He kind of does things on his own schedule."

McLeish stared, then shrugged. "Whatever. I'm just glad to get some help with this thing."

They paid the bill, McLeish insisting, then walked out to the sidewalk without speaking.

Zack turned to him. "Tell me, how did the FBI get involved in this? When you strip away the drama, it's a local murder case, isn't it?"

McLeish put a hand on Zack's arm. "Ah, glad you asked that. I forgot to mention the oil company. You see, high-pressure oil and gas pipelines run up the gorge right by the scene of the crime." He nodded toward the file under Zack's arm. "It's all there. The oil comes from offshore drilling platforms. The fire dancer story got some oil execs worried about the possibility of sabotage." McLeish grinned and shrugged. "So here we are."

During the drive home, Zack's mind returned to the mental images McLeish had presented. One thing was sure—whoever committed this crime made no attempt to conceal it. A fire at night in a dark canyon viewed by streams of motorists was meant to be seen. The body was meant to be found. It was a message. It was up to Zack to learn what that message was and for whom it was intended. The reports of the fiery dancing figure would need further investigation. There must be a connection. The fiery visions were like previews before the main feature film.

When Zack arrived home and told Libby he had accepted the case, she seemed relieved. While she didn't say it in so many words, Zack guessed he probably was getting on her nerves around the house. He was not good at idleness. The old place had been handed down from Libby's family, an old ranch in the wooded area just southeast of the Grand Canyon. Her great grandfather had built the homestead. The kitchen area had been the original blockhouse, protection against hostile Indians and outlaws. The family built on to it over the years so that it now sprawled across the slope. There was a large barn, where they kept horses and Libby's trained bloodhounds. When Zack first met Libby, it was through Big Blue, her best dog, on a manhunt. Big Blue had been involved in many of their cases, both before and after their marriage. She'd let the dog training go for a while after little Bernie was born, and spent most of her time with the baby. After that, there was the rough patch in their marriage, with Zack always away and Libby left alone with the child.

With his new title as Director of Special Cases, Zack's job description had changed in a way that allowed him the freedom to be home. He was now in a position to pick and choose his cases. He enjoyed being father and husband, puttering around, doing the patches on the roof, mending fences. But that life didn't challenge him, not in the way investigating crime had done. It didn't exhilarate him. Libby knew it.

The California case had come at a good time. Big Blue, long retired, had sired a very special pup, one which gave every sign of equaling if not surpassing it's sire's skills. Libby was very excited and about to plunge back into training. She'd be busy while Zack was away. Zack wouldn't need to worry about her as much.

His arrangements were set for tomorrow morning. His military flight out of Flagstaff would put him in Vandenberg by noon. His friend on the base had a Jeep ready for him. He'd meet McLeish in Lompoc in the early afternoon, then they'd head to the crime scene. Tonight Zack wanted to study the file, have it all in his head when he saw the scene of the crime for the first time.

Back at his desk, Zack flipped through the manila folder. Lying on top were several forensic photographs of a very badly burned woman. They showed her on her back, as she was when found. The metal hoops McLeish had mentioned were prominent in each photo, scorched and bent parabolas from her back to her face. The heat of the fire had fused them to her neck and face so that nothing remained of her features. Her arms were raised above her head, her legs and feet close together. Zack wondered if they had been tied. It was impossible to tell from the photos because the skin was gone in most places and curled and bubbled in others. The woman had not been fully cremated, but the fire had been extraordinarily hot.

Zack thought back to McLeish's description from the history, how the men investigating the 1864 murder had determined Mrs. Corliss was dragged by her feet into the house, thus causing the hoops, presumably smaller in diameter nearer the waist, to gather at her neck. As Zack studied the photos, he wondered if this woman had also been dragged to this position or had the hoops been carefully arranged before she was burned? The forensic report didn't mention drag marks.

Zack turned to Google, where he learned hoop skirts circa 1864 might have had as few as a dozen steel hoops or as many as forty, depending upon cost and style. He guessed that Mrs. Corliss, a woman married to a sheep farmer living in a rustic building in such a wild place must have opted for fewer hoops. She must have worn them to look dressier welcoming stagecoach guests.

How had the woman in these photos acquired a hoop skirt? A costume store? And why? Or had the murderer arranged for the dress and somehow put it on the deceased? Was this part of the message? The hoops had led McLeish and the local cops to study the history of the location. The hoops were the key to motive, Zack was sure.

There was a final manuscript in the manila file. Zack glanced at it, flipped through the pages. It was the story of Lucretia Corliss, as researched and recorded by an FBI clerk. Zack settled back in his chair and began to read.

CHAPTER THREE

Before the Whidby Island incident, Lucretia "Trecia" Corliss could not have been described as a fearful person. One doesn't cross an entire continent in a covered wagon on the Oregon Trail all the way from Ohio fording turbulent rivers, thirsting day after day while crossing hot, dry plains constantly alert for hostile Indians, either walking or riding on an unforgiving plank of a wagon seat for miles and miles and then at the end of all that carve out a home in the vast wilderness of Oregon Territory if you are not courageous. By the time George W. Corliss whisked her off to Olympia and marriage, the young woman had experienced more hardship and dangers than most do in a lifetime.

George had a half interest in a hotel in the growing town of Olympia, and at the time was serving as U.S. Marshal. He looked to the comfort of his new young wife, and they managed well despite the Indian War that erupted around them. The war was enacted in a scattered fashion, a kind of tit for tat "they killed ours, we'll kill theirs" sort of war. The settlements were spread out inland to coast and communication was undependable. It took a while for every inhabitant to know there was a war, and it took equally long to know if and when it had ended.

On his own passage across the plains, George became friends with Isaac N. Ebey, a man who settled on Whidby Island and later became a member of the Oregon Territory Legislative Assembly, the Island County's first Justice of the Peace, the local Postmaster, and the Customs Collector for the Puget Sound district. These offices conferred upon him great stature.

During a time when the Indian Wars were presumed to have ebbed, George had official business with the court located on Whidby Island and took advantage of his trip to bring Trecia along to visit with his old friend Isaac, Isaac's wife, and his two sons and a daughter.

That night at the Ebey home they were aroused by the violent barking of a dog. Col. Ebey went outside to investigate and shots sounded. He was seen at the window holding his head, seemingly dazed. More shots sounded and the people inside realized they were under attack by Indians. Having no firearms, they scattered out doors and windows and hid in the woods nearby. Trecia climbed out a window and leaped a fence, injuring herself in the process, but continued on up the road to the nearest neighbor. By the time she returned with help, Ebey's lifeless body lay upon the porch missing its head, which the Indians had carried off in triumph. They took it with them by canoe to their northern home near Port Gamble. It was a tit for tat killing, as it turned out, in revenge for an Indian of high stature killed by cannon fire.

Despite her heroics in running for help, Trecia never completely recovered from the incident and carried with her a deathly fear of American Indians. A friend who visited her some months later observed her still on crutches and in a highly nervous state. When George's term as U.S. Marshal ended in 1860, he sold his interest in the hotel and moved his wife to a pleasant community on the outskirts of the burgeoning city of Olympia. Despite his care, Trecia's nerves showed no sign of recovering. George concluded their only option was to depart the area and seek solace on a sheep farm he acquired in Las Cruces, Santa Barbara County, California, a tiny community just north of the Gaviota Gap, a rocky narrow defile through the barrier rampart of the Santa Ynez Mountains. They built their home in the valley above the gorge and grazed their sheep on the abundant grasses covering the lower slopes of the mountains on either side. Their nearest neighbors lived in the old Las Cruces Adobe a mile or so north and on the Gaviota Rancho south and east of the Gap. In the months that followed, Trecia overcame her fears. Her letters home spoke of a peaceful, happy existence. She urged her aging parents in Oregon to join them in Las Cruces. "You know how afraid I always was in Olympia," she wrote. "I have gotten all over that now."'

More good fortune came their way when the stagecoach company decided to change their station to a location north of the Gap. Bids went up. The stage station proprietorship would mean extra money; lots of it. George and Lucretia Corliss won the bid and soon were in the stage station business. For those who bid and lost, there was unhappiness and resentment. The unsuccessful bidders included the three Williams brothers, residents of the Las Cruces Adobe. They had been so certain of success they built a barn to house the stagecoach horses. No less unhappy were the Cotas, their neighbors to the south, who lost the contract because of the move away from them. When on February 16, 1864, the stagecoach made its daily stop at the Corliss station, they found it burnt down. Inside the charred ruins were the murdered bodies of George and Lucretia Corliss. Investigators were able to determine through bloody handprints and other indications that Lucretia Corliss had once again escaped out a window but this time was subsequently caught and dragged back into the building where she died. Investigators found the door had been locked from the outside, presumably to prevent escape from the flames, suggesting either or both of the victims might still have been alive."

Zack sat back and breathed deeply. What a poignant yet horrific story! Such an event as this might well live on in the mind of descendants and serve as a motive for a crime today. That would be something to check out.

Zack picked up the phone.

"Hey."

"Hey yourself, White Man."

"I've got a job in California, Central Coast. Place called Las Cruces. You may remember the area. Flying over tomorrow. You in?"

"Yes. I will meet you there."

Zack hung up, grinning. Eagle Feather was always ready to go.

At six a.m. the next morning, Zack's friend Spud from Vandenberg called him to tell him of a cargo flight departing Tuba City Airport flying directly to Vandenberg. It would be much more convenient for Zack.

"In Tuba City? What on earth for?"

Spud laughed. "Go figger, right? It's imaging equipment for satellites. They've been experimenting in your vast open spaces out there trying to enhance satellite image focus with some sort of ground radar they drop in by drone, theoretically into an enemy position. Gives them that Google Street look effect that the satellite controller can manipulate."

"So they just happen to be packing it up today?"

"You're one lucky SOB. Yeah, I've booked you on it. Leaves Tuba City at noon. You should show up no later than half past eleven."

Zack quickly called Flagstaff and canceled his commercial flight. He grinned. He could now leave home three hours later than planned and he'd actually arrive in Vandenberg earlier. Not bad.

* * * * *

When Zack walked down the ramp of the C17 Globemaster he immediately saw the relaxed figure of Spud Jarvis leaning against a red Jeep Cherokee, his long legs crossed, his blond hair wrapped in a red kerchief, his camouflage T-shirt tucked into Airborne vintage pants, watching Zack cross the hot tarmac.

"You are overdressed, seems to me," Spud said, putting out a hand.

Zack glanced down at the heavy hoody he wore. "Saves packing an extra bag. I'll peel it off first chance."

Spud handed Zack a guest identity badge. Zack took it. He glanced at the Cherokee. "This for me?"

"Yup. Got it on loan from a friend. He's on a mission, won't need it for a month."

Zack smiled. "Hope I'll be long gone by then."

"Where you headed first?"

"I got to meet Agent McLeish in Lompoc at three."

"You got lots of time. Hop in. We'll go get a beer and catch up."

Spud drove off the tarmac and through several gates where he was waved ahead. They headed to the Pacific Coast Club. There they ate at the bar, enjoying a burger and a beer.

"Not bad," Zack said. "Seems like a nice cozy life you've got here."

Spud chuckled. "It's got its moments."

Zack had met Spud at the Academy where he was taking supplementary training for his security work with the Air Force, which included keeping an eye on nukes. Spud rose quickly through the AFOSI (Air Force Office of Special Investigations) due to his easy-going manner and intense loyalty. Zack had been drawn to him for the same reasons.

"Can you tell me what you're working on?" Spud asked, licking the Firestone IPA froth from his lips.

Zack gave him a quick rundown.

"Sounds spooky, especially the fire dance bit. Wonder how they did that?" Spud said.

Zack gave him a sideways look. "You don't believe it was the ghost of the murdered woman appearing after one hundred fifty years, apparently."

Spud laughed. "Not hardly. The question to me is not how, but why? Why go to all that trouble to broadcast the murder?"

"Maybe somebody thinks justice wasn't done back then and needs to be redressed now."

Spud shook his head. "Just as likely somebody is aware of the history and planned all that drama in this way to throw people like you off the track. Might have nothing to do with anything."

Zack shrugged. "I thought of that, too."

"But if you want to see ghosts, you won't be disappointed, I'm told. They say the old Adobe is attended by at least four ghosts—three prostitutes still trying to ply their trade and a gunfighter with a knee-length black coat and a wide-brimmed hat." He chuckled. "Never heard of a fiery ghost dancing, though."

Zack gave a sheepish grin. "All ghost stories aside, there was a murder and apparently we are missing suspects, motive, and even the identity of the victim."

CHAPTER FOUR

Spud escorted Zack out to the Vandenberg gate where the two men shook hands and agreed to meet again soon. Zack was in time to join McLeish at the Starbucks in Lompoc as arranged. The two FBI agents grabbed coffees to go. Zack followed McLeish's white pickup through town and south on Route 1 through the Santa Ynez Mountains. The spring rains were a recent memory, the hills rose on his left with the emerald freshness of an Irish landscape while on his right a river course at the base of the mountains nurtured large twisted oak and occasional stands of pine. After a few miles, the flanking mountains steepened, their slopes tangled with chaparral and crowned with outbursts of fractured rock. A sense of wildness prevailed here. On the final long descent into the Las Cruces Valley, Zack's feeling of the coldness and desolation of the area increased.

Just before the junction with the Hwy 101, they turned off onto a side road, drove past a school building of stucco and Spanish tile and pulled into a parking lot next to a deserted but substantial restroom building.

McLeish came over to the Cherokee as Zack climbed out and stretched. "Caltrans built this when they planned to put in a highway rest stop here," McLeish said. "Funding ran out and they deserted the project. The Adobe is over this way."

Zack followed him along a wide path and over a footbridge. They came to a panel of display signs, the Plexiglas protection scratched and scarred. Beyond the signs was a tall wire fence surrounding what at first glance appeared to be mud walls and rubble.

McLeish continued his explanation. "You see, the whole plan was to highlight the Las Cruces Adobe and the history of the region. But this is as far as they got. When the project ended, they threw a cover over the building and fenced it in to keep out vandals."

They walked through the tall grass toward the building.

"You got to keep a roof on an adobe building to preserve it, otherwise the weather will take it down in no time. As you can see, much of the original roof has collapsed and some walls have too, but you can get the idea of the old building."

"What was the original plan for it?" Zack asked.

"I believe they intended to reconstruct the building and the adjacent barn there. But as you can see..." McLeish shrugged.

Zack walked along the fence, peering in. If anything, the ruin increased the sense of isolation and wildness of the area. "This is where the brothers lived?"

"The Williams brothers. Yeah, that's right. They built that barn there just for the stage horses."

"And the murder site?"

"Down canyon. We'll go that way next."

McLeish's phone rang. He spoke for a moment, put it away. "Great timing. Our rides are here," he said.

Zack raised his eyebrows.

McLeish grinned. "You ride horseback, don't you?"

"Of course."

They reached the top of the rise where the walkway met the parking lot. A large horse trailer drawn by a pickup truck was just entering the lot.

"I thought it might be a good idea to give you a perspective on the original murder and early history along with the topography and current political situation. We can do that from up there." McLeish gestured toward the top of the mountain that rose in front of them.

A cowboy waved and walked to the rear of the trailer. They went toward him as they talked.

"The Rancho San Julian was kind enough to loan us a couple of mounts for our little jaunt today."

Zack watched as the cowboy lowered the trailer ramp, disappeared inside and reappeared leading a horse. The mount was saddled and ready to go. The cowboy handed the reigns to McLeish.

"Thanks, Jeb," McLeish said and handed the reins to Zack. "This is your mount. Best check the stirrups and give the saddle a cinch."

Zack checked over the setup as Jeb reappeared with McLeish's mount. McLeish had gone to his vehicle for water bottles. He gave one to Zack and turned his attention to his own horse.

The two men mounted up.

"We'll see you in a couple of hours," McLeish told Jeb, and they rode down the pavement side by side.

McLeish waved an arm in the direction they were headed. "We're nearing the Gaviota Gorge entrance up here. Everything narrows and funnels into it. It's a fault. The bedrock rose at a crazy angle and snapped the spine of the mountain range just here. The water rushing through over the eons did the rest. We'll get a good view higher up."

They passed a couple of cars parked along the side and came to a locked state park gate, meant to prohibit automobiles but not pedestrians and equestrians. They rode around it, passing the ubiquitous mountain lion warning sign. The trail was the width of a carriageway, imprinted by the feet and hooves of many hikers and riders. They rode past another Plexiglas display at a trail juncture.

"That's the trail map. The Ortega trail departs there. We'll come back to it later."

Their track steepened immediately, paralleling a high ridge on their right. To the left, a spectacular view of the gorge gradually opened. They crossed a small ridge and dropped down into an arroyo filled with old growth oak trees. Zack had never seen anything like these trees. Some had branches almost two feet thick that snaked fifty feet or more across the ravine, sometimes intertwining with similar branches from other trees. Except where the road cut, it was a dark, deep and mysterious place, where water trickled somewhere below. Zack caught glimpses of vales with tall green grass, guarded by monster trees and tangled by fallen branches and uprooted tree trunks.

"My god."

McLeish nodded. "Yeah, it is impressive. I wouldn't want to lose a heifer down in there."

The trail crossed the arroyo and lifted them up and out the other side and they switched back toward the east angling up the side of a ridge. Zack looked down at the Arroyo, now just the green tops of oak trees guarding the secret that lay beneath. From here, they could look out across the larger valley to the high peaks of the Santa Ynez mountains on the other side. Zack heard a truck air-brake on the 101 Freeway as they descended into the gorge.

They reached the ridgeline at a large oak tree. Under it, the trail swung west again and ascended the slope. McLeish dismounted and walked his horse to the far edge of the ridge. Zack followed.

The view here was God-like. When McLeish began explaining, Zack stopped him. He could not assimilate what he was seeing so quickly.

"Wait! That"—he pointed— "is the Pacific Ocean?"

"Yes."

"But what are those mountains beyond it?"

"Those are the Channel Islands."

"They just seem to be floating out there."

"That's the effect of the fog, and the distance."

"Are those ships?" Zack saw several objects in the ocean between the land and the islands.

"Those are offshore oil platforms. They are part of the political story."

"And right here, where the cars are going, the tunnel, that's the Gaviota Gorge?"

McLeish nodded. "That's right."

"There's just room for the highway through there."

"Wasn't even that much room back in the day before they carved out the tunnel and dynamited the lower course. Back then, at its narrowest, there was barely room for two horsemen to pass one another."

Zack glanced at McLeish. "That's pretty tight."

McLeish grinned. "No doubt about it. There's the story of a known and wanted outlaw and a county sheriff who met right in the middle and kept riding pretending neither recognized the other. Outlaws hung about this area like fleas on a dog." He waved an arm. "Part of the problem was distance. In the 1850s and 60s, the closest places to the gorge were the ranchos. Since most were owned by Mexicans still filled with rancor from the war, Americans couldn't necessarily expect support. Santa Barbara is still thirty miles away in that direction, Santa Ynez Mission is twenty miles in that direction, and La Purisima Mission is over twenty miles in that direction." McLeish swung his arm in a circle pausing at three, ten, and one o'clock to explain. "When a robbery or other crimes occurred here, the perpetrator was gone and the victim dead and buried before anything resembling law could get here. The Corliss murder wasn't discovered until the next day when the stage came through. The posse from Santa Barbara didn't show up for another day after that."

"Where was the Corliss cabin?"

"No one seems to know, exactly. I haven't found any accurate descriptions. But I have a hunch someone knows." McLeish pointed down at the gorge. "See where the northbound lanes exit the tunnel and begin a wide sweeping turn? Right there is where motorists have claimed to see the fiery dancing figure somewhere out in front of them. Now draw a straight line from the center of that curve across the ravine. See those grassy places? That's where the body was found, and I believe that's where the Corliss cabin once stood."

"Not much else down there looks level enough for a residence," Zack said.

"That's true. The Williams brothers kept a horse corral along there somewhere and sheep grazed all over the lower slopes, but the only sensible location for a cabin and barn to my eye has to be there."

"Can we take a look?"

"Sure enough. But first, now that you've got the topographical perspective, let me give you the political one." McLeish nodded toward the Pacific Ocean. "Those oil rigs you spotted pipe the crude they pump along the seabed to a place out of sight around that headland there to the east. There they remove gasses and lighten it enough to pipe it to distribution and refining locations. Several pipelines come up this valley. A couple of them cross up and over that summit ridge in front of us." He pointed to the right. "One stays up on that ridge above us headed north." His arm moved to point below them. "Another high volume high-pressure pipeline drops down and runs just west of the creek, right through that green area."

"The old Corliss place?"

"I believe so."

"So a fiery spectacle above an area where a high-pressure pipeline runs—"

"Is why you and I are standing here and not just the local cops."

"I can see the reason for concern."

"Especially since the company that owns the pipeline had a large spill in recent memory, so recent that they are looking for permission to replace the old pipeline with a new one. That request stirred up the question of the safety record of this particular company." He answered Zack's raised eyebrows. "Not a good one."

"So our fire dancer ratchets up the alarm."

McLeish nodded. "Which could be another motive."

Zack narrowed his eyes at McLeish. "A motive to create the fiery figure, maybe, but for murder?"

McLeish shrugged. "Who knows how far some protesters might go?" He reached over to pat his horse's neck, preparing to mount. "So that's about it from up here. Any questions before we go down to the murder site?"

"Just one," Zack said. "Why the hell would anyone chose to live in such a desolate place?"

They retraced their route down the steep road to the junction with the Ortega Trail. Here McLeish took the lead. It was a narrow trail, just a path, often overgrown by tall grasses and intruding brush. Once or twice Zack had to hug his horse's neck to avoid low tree branches. They crossed jagged rents in the soft soil carved by storm water rushing down from the upper slopes, leaving boulders and thick chunks of oak branches in its wake. Then the trail climbed a knoll and at the top McLeish reigned in and dismounted. A wall of pitted sandstone guarded the uphill side and slickrock sloped off gradually to the other side. From this vantage, Zack could see beyond to the walls forming the narrow gorge, and the mountain slopes that rose precipitously across the valley. In between, hidden from view, he heard the growling of trucks and the roar of traffic. Around them were occasional oak trees, so large and gnarled Zack guessed they must be hundreds of years old.

"This is it," McLeish said. "We'll tie the horses here and I'll show you around.

Yellow barricade tape was festooned above the rock face and continued on along the uphill side of the path. Zack followed McLeish a few yards back the way they had come where they turned off the path to climb a steep grassy slope. Clumps of grass and unstable rock gave way beneath their feet. After a short but strenuous climb up loosened sod clumps and over oak branches, they came to an open space of tall grass. More tape surrounded a level area just beyond the cliff edge. A tall slender man in jeans and a flannel shirt, arms crossed, dark hair neatly combed, stood watching them approach.

McLeish's response was immediate. "Who are you? What are you doing here? This is a crime scene."

The man smiled quietly. He wore an air of quiet confidence. "I fully understand that. I have the authorization to inspect the scene." He took a step toward them. "You must be Agent McLeish. You are the only official I have not yet met." He reached in his shirt pocket and brought out a plastic card. "Here is my identification and authorization. My name is John Halligon. I represent the oil company that owns the pipeline that lies beneath your feet." He handed the card to McLeish.

The agent glanced at it, handed it back and shook Halligon's hand. "Nice to meet you. This is FBI Agent Zack Tolliver, Director of Special Cases. He is assisting me."

Halligon shook Zack's hand as well. He had a firm grip and a pleasant manner. He gestured toward the area beyond the tape. "Not much to see there."

McLeish shook his head. "No, with the body removed, there's nothing but some scorched grass." He shook his head. "Funny how the flames never got out of control, almost as if the killer stood here with a tool of some sort to prevent it."

Zack walked the few steps up to the tape and gazed at the area it enclosed. "Seems like bedrock just beneath the turf here. You say you think Corliss built a cabin here?"

McLeish shrugged. "Can't say it was exactly there. Might have been farther up the slope there. Or the subfloor could have been anchored to the rock." He squinted at the oil man. "How was your pipeline laid through here?"

Halligon shook his head. "Couldn't come through here. We brought it just upslope of here through a rift in the underlying ledge."

"Agent McLeish tells me you plan to lay new pipe. Where will that run?" Zack asked.

Halligon frowned. "We can't answer that yet. We think we can improve upon the current location, make it safer. But to do that we need to procure a lot more permits for the right of way, involving the state, county, private ownership, various conservation groups, and, of course, the Chumash, who have burials and ceremonial sites all through this area."

"Wasn't the anthropological research done for this area?" McLeish asked.

"Well, we thought so." Halligon shrugged. "But tribal members complained that members of the research committee were pro-oil, untrained, or generally lacked knowledge." He grinned. "Happily, that's not my assignment. My job is to see to the security of the present pipeline. Just imagine if someone sabotaged it in the current political environment. There'd be no chance to obtain permits in that case."

"You think this burning may be some kind of message?" Zack asked.

"Not the murder. I mean, Christ! I hope not. But the flaming figure motorists reported could be."

McLeish looked at the oil man. "Don't you think the flaming figure must be connected to this murder?"

"You're the crime solvers. We need you to tell us," he said, grinning.

McLeish glanced at Zack. "I guess we better get at it, then." He nodded at Halligon. "Nice to meet you."

Halligon waved and climbed with agile grace down the slope. Zack and McLeish turned their attention to the area confined by the police tape.

"I assume the body was in that area I see surrounded by scorched grass," Zack said.

McLeish nodded. "The area there—"

The crack of a rifle sounded, sharp, unmistakable, with immediate reverberation re-echoing among the hills. Both men instinctively dropped into the tall grass. Zack waited, unable to see McLeish or much else beyond the spikes of the grasses waving gently above his eye level. He tried to orient the sound of the shot in his mind. He thought it had come from the opposite side of the valley, but the echo made it difficult to tell.

"McLeish, are you okay?" he whispered.

A muffled "Yeah" came in reply. "You?"

"I'm okay. If we were the target, it was a wide miss."

Silence. Then, louder, "Halligon, you okay?" from McLeish.

There was silence for long seconds. Then they heard the exclamation, "Shit!"

"Halligon?"

"I'm okay, but the tree where I was just standing has a chunk missing."

CHAPTER FIVE

"Stay down, don't move," Zack called out, then spoke softly to McLeish. "We've got to get off this hilltop, try to get an eye on the shooter. The shot had to come from below or across the valley. This cliff shelters Halligon from above. You work your way forward to where you have some cover and can see out. I'll go back the other way. Put your phone on vibrate and we'll message."

"Got it."

Zack began to worm his way back through the tall grass, trying to move gently to create a pattern to simulate wind in the grass tips. Ten minutes later he was on the downward slope toward the trail. Here he could move between trees and boulders. When the trail came into view, he saw the oilman just off the trail flat on his stomach behind a log. Halligon's head turned incrementally to squint up at Zack.

Zack waved him stay down, finger on lips. He studied the terrain beneath them, slowly working his way along the bullet's possible trajectory across the valley and then up the opposite slopes. There was a whole lot of territory to cover. He saw nothing. He messaged McLeish. "Anything?"

His reply came. "Could be anywhere."

"Suggestions?"

"I'm calling in air cover now."

They hollered to Halligon to stay down and waited. Zack could shift position occasionally to ease muscle ache. He felt sorry for Halligon, who had no way to ease his cramps without exposing himself. It was twenty minutes before the helicopter arrived. It hovered over the highway, a few hundred feet away. The propeller wash set the tree branches around them dancing.

Zack's phone vibrated. He pushed up the volume. "Yeah?"

"Zack, the men in the helicopter don't see anybody, but they will hold their position until we are clear of this area. Let's check the horses."

Zack scrambled down and gave the news to Halligon, who had already gotten to his feet, trembling with stiff muscles. His shirt was partially untucked with leaves embedded around his belt. He showed Zack where he had been standing when the bullet struck the tree. It had been very close.

The horses were fine, although skittish. McLeish rode double with Halligon and they rode back along the pathway, escorted by the helicopter several hundred feet away. They reached the park gate without further incident.

Halligon was clearly stressed by the close call. He almost fell dismounting McLeish's horse. He was sweating despite the cool breeze.

"Where is your vehicle?" McLeish asked.

Halligon pointed at a small white sedan with a logo on the door.

Zack dismounted, handed the reigns to McLeish, and walked around the car, then looked under it. "No obvious problems. Are you okay to drive? We can give you a ride, you can pick the car up tomorrow."

"Why would anyone want to kill me?"

"They meant to kill somebody," Zack said. "That was too close for a warning shot. The question is, did they know who they were trying to kill?"

"Like maybe it was me they wanted," McLeish said to Halligon. "You'd already been there. The guy didn't shoot until after we arrived."

"Or me," Zack said. "I'm the new guy around here."

Halligon seemed to relax a bit. "Well, that's better, then."

The other two men raised eyebrows.

"No, no, I mean it's better than if—oh hell, you know what I mean."

Zack patted him on his shoulder and grinned. "We know what you mean. But we all need to take precautions from now on."

Halligon fished car keys out of his pocket. "I'll tell you one thing. I'm not doing anything else with this pipeline until the company assigns me a security guard or two." Once they were safe, McLeish sent the helicopter to reconnoiter. Its presence might keep the marksman pinned down for a while. Zack figured they might have time to catch him on the move once the helicopter departed. They discussed it while Jeb reloaded the horses into the trailer. They'd soon be at their barn for a nice rubdown.

"How do we get to the other side of the valley where the shooter is?" Zack asked.

"Follow me," McLeish said.

Zack followed the agent's white truck out the access road onto Route 1. In minutes they had crossed the freeway and were on a similar access road on the opposite side of the canyon that came to an end at a turnaround. As Zack climbed out of the Cherokee he could hear the helicopter buzzing along the mountainside. Several cars were parked near them.

McLeish opened his car trunk and removed a holstered weapon, checked its load, and belted it on before sliding a light jacket on to conceal it.

Zack's 9mm Glock rested in his shoulder holster under a thick wool shirt he'd worn on the plane. He wore it as a light jacket, but even so, it felt warm in the California sunshine. He followed McLeish to a large signpost by the trailhead.

The agent put a finger on the acrylic over the map and traced a line. "This is the main trail. Other trails depart it after a few tenths of a mile, right here. First, the Trespass trail breaks away to the right headed south. Next, the Hot Springs Trail follows the stream another tenth of a mile. The main trail turns north but makes a long swing upslope and turns back on itself on its way to the summit of Gaviota Peak.

The map showed contours and was easy to follow.

"But our man must have been over here somewhere," Zack said, indicating an area to the south.

"Right. To get there from here, he'd follow the Trespass Trail. Then, likely the Underpass trail, where it takes a lower course along the slope."

"What range are we talking about here?' Zack asked. "That was a pretty damn good shot."

"Much closer than it seems. From the Underpass Trail, his shot is no more than a quarter mile. The Trespass Trail parallels above it. He could find a shot from there of less than a half mile."

Zack thought about it. "Over eight hundred yards would require specialized equipment and training beyond the average rifleman, which narrows the hunt. Half that, however, puts the shot within the skill zone of most practiced hunters with a good rifle and scope. Given the percentages, that's the most likely scenario, wouldn't you say?"

McLeish nodded. "I'll go with that."

"Is there any way to get there other than this trail system?"

"Quite a few, unfortunately. First, he can move out along the Tunnel View Trail until it meets the Trespass Trail, then continue on up the ravine. At the saddle, he can go almost anywhere, either up Gaviota Peak and out along the ridgeline, continue on down the other side of the saddle to meet trails coming up various arroyos that lead to the freeway, or climb the southern ridge and drop down on the oil refining facility."

Zack's head jerked up at that. "If he's associated with the oil company, would that be his route?"

McLeish shrugged. "From what I've learned, it's not the easiest route and it's exposed. The helicopter would spot him up there easily unless he waits for dark."

"Where else could he go?"

"He could drop down to the southbound rest area. There's an underpass he can reach from the trail. That will bring him to the freeway just above the rest area. He could walk along the road or try to follow the creek."

"So his car could be among fifty others parked there."

McLeish nodded. "That's the way I would go. Take my shot, sprint down the trail, walk along the freeway shoulder and throw my rifle in the back seat. At that point, I could relax, go take a pee, and be any other tourist traveling through."

"But not while the helicopter is flying."

"Right."

Zack looked at his watch. "I'll stay here. You go down to where the trail meets the highway above the rest stop. Once you are in position, send the helicopter higher on the mountain in case the shooter tries that escape. How much longer do you have the bird?"

McLeish was walking away. "Another hour. I'll come back here after that." He jumped in his car and spun off, flinging dirt.

Zack re-parked his car, positioning it to keep the trail and the empty cars in view. He wrote down the license plate numbers of the cars. After that he sat quietly, letting his mind play over the events of the last hours. The topographic relief lines on the trail display map suggested a man could set up near the junction of the Tunnel View and Underpass trails and have a straight shot of between six and seven hundred yards. The wind would play a part, but there wasn't much today.

His musing was interrupted when a man emerged from the woods at the trailhead. He was a big man, heavyset, wearing a backpack, felt hat and hiking boots. He had a weary look. His eyes were fixed on the cars and moved toward one of them. Zack stepped out and walked to him.

"Howdy. You look like you've been out there a while."

The man glanced at him, gave a weary smile. "Two days. Camped out near the pond water in the saddle below Gaviota Peak."

"I'm new here, thinking I'd like to do some hiking up there. Is it difficult?"

The man shrugged. "Not really, take your time. Lots of uphill one way, a lot of downhill the other." He stepped to his car, remotely opened the trunk. Zack glanced in. Other than some clothing, another pair of shoes, there was little else. The man shrugged off his backpack and dropped it in.

"If you want the real experience, go high," he said. "It's hard to match the views you'll find up there." He slammed the trunk closed, climbed in the driver's seat, started up the car with the door still open. Just before he closed it, Zack stepped in the way of it.

"Did you happen to hear a shot about a half hour ago?"

The man rubbed his fingers through thick black hair. "You know, now you mention it, I did hear something like a gunshot as I was descending. Came from somewhere below me. At first, I thought it was a truck backfire, but it was sharper, more percussive." He glanced up at Zack. "Why? Did something happen?"

Zack studied his face for a moment, stepped back. "Just curious. Didn't think hunting was allowed out here." He closed the man's door and watched him drive away. The backpack seemed too small for a rifle and scope, even disassembled. In any case, he had the car license number and could identify the man if necessary. He walked back to the Cherokee.

He waited. The sun warmed his windshield and forced him to remove the shirt, despite the open windows. Two young children, both girls, frolicked forth from the trail, their mom appearing minutes later draped with towels. They'd apparently been to the hot springs. They climbed into a Land Rover and soon drove away. Two cars remained.

Zack realized he no longer could hear the helicopter. This was affirmed when his phone buzzed.

"The bird's gone," McLeish said. "If he's gonna move, it'll be now. Anything your end?"

"Nothing."

"Okay, we wait."

Zack had a long sip from the water bottle, thankful McLeish had thought to give it to him. It was growing quite warm in the Cherokee, but he didn't want to turn on the engine and air conditioning and make it obvious he was waiting. He glanced at his watch. It was nearly four. The sun was at its hottest angle, but close to the mountain ridge. He'd be a lot cooler soon, but it would get dark rapidly in this narrow valley.

He eyed the two parked cars. One was a Mini Cooper, an unlikely seeming transport for an assassin, but who knew? The other was a big Chevy SUV, black with darkened windows. The obvious choice. But again...

When the shadows came, they were long and dark, contrasting sharply with sunlit spaces. It was difficult to see detail within them. Half his car was now in the shadow of a nearby tree. The cooling effect came quickly.

There was motion. Something just beyond the brush at the trailhead. Something moving rapidly, now still as if listening. Waiting.

Zack lifted the Glock from the holster, lay it on his lap, watched.

Movement again, remarkably swift, but away, gone.

Zack swore under his breath, pushed open the door, jumped out. He stood, listened. Had the sniper seen him? Was he even now running back up the trail into the darkness? Zack would have to cross the open parking area to find out.

He'd make a perfect target.

The movement came again, no paused this time, straight into the open right at Zack. He raised his pistol.

He pulled up his arm just in time. The dog, a black Lab, came right up to greet him, licked the other hand Zack offered. A large woman leaning heavily on a walking stick stood at the edge of the parking area.

"He's just real friendly," she said, annoyed. "You don't have to shoot him. What's the matter with you, anyway."

CHAPTER SIX

The black SUV was gone now, only the Mini Cooper remained. The woman with the dog had been only slightly mollified by Zack's explanations and credentials. She had not heard any sound resembling a shot. She saw no justification for pointing a gun at her dog "even if you were president." He heard her grumbling right up until her door closed.

Zack glanced at his watch. It was four-thirty, over half an hour since the helicopter had departed. It would be a lot darker in another hour. If their man was coming this way, he'd have to come soon. If the Mini belonged to him, he might even now be looking down on him, wondering who owned the Cherokee. Zack slumped lower in the seat. One thing stood in his favor; the license plate on the Jeep was out of state—Alabama if he recalled correctly. Spud's friend must have been relocated to Vandenberg from there. That happened a lot, he knew. That should allay the suspicions of the shooter to some degree.

The shadows deepened. His phone buzzed.

"It's pretty damn dark and cold down here," McLeish said. "Anything happening up there?"

"Just one car left in the lot. All the others have gone. There were no likely suspects, but I've got the plate numbers and vehicle models just in case. I had a chance to shoot someone's pet dog but didn't take it."

There was a pause. "That's just as well, I guess. Zack, take a look at the dash of that last car. See if there is a ticket there. Some people camp overnight up in the mountains. They pay a fee and leave the ticket stub where it can be seen."

"Hang on." Zack climbed out of the Cherokee and walked to the Mini. Sure enough, on the broad dash behind the large windshield was a ticket stub. It looked official. "Yeah, there's one here."

"Okay, let's give it up. You've got the plate number. I think that's all we can do for now. That was a CHP copter we just borrowed.

They've agreed to have troopers keep an eye on possible escape avenues, and an investigative team will go in tomorrow to try to find evidence. How about some dinner? There's a place down the road in Buellton called A.J. Spurs that serves a pretty nice steak."

Zack was shivering. He couldn't believe it could get this cold this fast. "I'll drive up to the head of the access road and meet you there."

They drove in tandem on the 101 to the Buellton exit. At shortly after five, they were a bit ahead of the dinner crowd and just in time for Happy Hour. McLeish engineered a table a bit away from the others and once drinks were in hand, they settled back to talk about the case.

"You had a chance to read the history in the file?" McLeish asked.

Zack nodded. "Real sad story. Kind of ironic."

"They never found the killers, as I said. They let the Williams brothers off for lack of evidence. Some say Mexican Bandits did it, others say the Williams boys got away with murder."

"How is the story relevant to this murder?"

"Well, that's the question, isn't it?" McLeish sipped his drink. "I've got something else for you since we last met." He pulled a folded set of papers out of his pocket. "This here is the coroner's report. I'll let you read it."

Zack took the familiar forms, read through them. McLeish waited. Zack flipped a page, looked up in surprise. "It wasn't hoops from a skirt fused to her face. Those were adjustment bands for a staved barrel."

McLeish grinned. "Right. Plenty of those around here with the wineries. This guy simply used the tools at hand to make his point."

"His point being to mimic the hoop skirt from the original murder."

"Seems so."

"Any way to trace these bands to a particular winery?"

"No chance. With dozens of wineries in the region, not to speak of beer brewers who use similar barrels, there must be thousands of these generic adjustment bands being supplied."

Zack read on. "I see you asked about facial reconstruction."

"They told me no chance of that because the bone structure of the face was deformed by the melting hoops."

Zack grunted. "Almost as if planned."

"Yeah. And of course they can get DNA, but without somewhere to start looking for a match, that's a dead end."

Zack lifted an eyebrow. "No missing white female"—he glanced at the first page—"between forty and fifty years of age, five feet five inches tall, no broken bones or other identifying characteristics."

McLeish laughed. "Not much to go on. There are no missing persons at all in the immediate area in recent weeks. Of course, nearer the big cities, LA or San Francisco there are. But that"—he pointed at the forensic report—"just doesn't give us enough. We can't even tell the race of the victim."

"That must have been a very hot fire."

"Indeed."

"As if the intent was to hide the identity of the victim."

McLeish nodded.

Zack went on thinking out loud. "This murder must have happened at night. As I now know, it gets pretty cold at night in that canyon, which means his fire needs to be even hotter. What accelerant did he use to burn that body so thoroughly?"

"You know, Zack, that is an excellent question. The lab is working on it, but they don't have an answer yet. They did say it wasn't gasoline or propane or any common, readily available fuel."

The waitress arrived with two large steaming plates. Zack's sirloin was so large part hung over the plate to make room for the baked potato. The two men set to work without delay.

After a pause to chew McLeish nodded toward the report next to Zack's plate. "You'll notice in the findings their belief most of the burning occurred off-site.

"I wondered about that myself," Zack said. "There did not appear to be sufficient damage to the site for the temperature required to burn her so thoroughly and melt the hoops."

McLeish, busy chewing, nodded.

Zack put his fork down. "So if this is simply a ruse to conceal the victim's identity, it must be with the assumption a lot of people know the history of the original murders. Is that true?"

McLeish swallowed his food. "Generally, no. I didn't know and the local cops didn't know."

"So what got you on to it?"

"A park ranger who knew a bit about it. He mentioned it and we did the research."

"That's right! I'd forgotten that area is a state park. The murderer would expect this history to come to light."

"I suppose so."

"Leaving us with the question, was the placement of the body meant to reference the history or to use the history to help obscure the identity of the victim and sow confusion?"

McLeish wiped his mouth with his napkin. "And if the body was burned off-site, as we suspect, where could that be done? The woman was practically cremated."

Zack stared at him. "Just so."

McLeish stared back. "Right. I'll begin checking out crematoriums in the morning."

"Let me know what the county sheriff learns about the shooter today. I'd love to know who he thought he was shooting at, an oil man, feds, or what?"

McLeish nodded as he took another bite. "If he knew he was trying to shoot an oil man, we may have a whole other motive for placing the body there."

Zack leaned back in his chair. "Tell me more about the oil situation around here."

The agent sighed. "Where to begin? Oil here is as old as...well, as old as the hills." He grinned. "Because of a geological tilt, the oil layers surface and seep out right off the beach at Gaviota."

"Below the gorge."

"That's right. The Native Americans used the tar to seal their Tomols, their big ocean-going canoes. Then the Spanish came and used it to seal the roofs of their adobes. They knew every place where the asphaltum or brea, as they called it, bubbled up. As the country began to industrialize, the demand for the stuff grew exponentially and this county was the center of it all. The oil boom in Central California slowed on occasions but never really stopped. Big Oil sucked up the underground pools and moved to other easy diggings but have returned as those were emptied. The Monterey Shale layer under our feet holds untold amounts of crude, but it's all mixed in with the sandstone and hard to extract. So they've developed these techniques to shock or steam it loose. The shock method, hydraulic fracturing it's called, got banned in this county because the potential negative impact on the environment. Some say it causes earthquakes." McLeish grinned. "People here are a little shy of earthquakes."

"And the steam method?"

"Steam Injection also uses a lot of water, but the oil companies have been underplaying that. I've heard an engineer say it takes almost as much energy to steam heat the rock as the oil it releases can produce." McLeish shrugged. "Wouldn't know about that."

Zack gave a slow shake of his head. "Where do things stand now?"

"Pretty much where things stand everywhere. We've got a pro-oil administration, ready to pull apart parks and monuments and oceans or anything else that may have oil under it." McLeish took a sip from his water glass. "Here in Santa Barbara County, we've got oil companies on grounds they've worked since the industry began that want to drill hundreds of more wells. But things aren't the same as they were a century and a half ago. Agriculture, particularly vineyards, has grown astronomically in the valleys. In recent climate conditions, we've seen aquifers nearly go dry As one oil spokesperson said, oil is a messy business. There have been many spills over the years and hundreds of violations by the oil companies. People here are afraid they'll lose their precious water resources. It wouldn't take much."

"And Gaviota Gorge?"

The agent pushed his chair back from the table, sat back and crossed his arms. "Ah, the gorge. Well, I pointed out the pipelines to you today. All those offshore rigs you saw funnel the oil to the gorge area. The pipeline company had a big spill recently, as I told you. So they want to rebuild it, make it better. They want it to last forever. People around here aren't so sure they want the oil industry around that long. The kind of development on the part of the oil companies I've been talking about is a huge investment. It doesn't suggest there is a plan to work toward alternate energy sources."

Zack smiled. "It's been my experience when it comes to environmental issues there are two kinds of people. There are the Here And Now thinkers and the Tomorrow is Coming Sooner Than You Think thinkers. It's a pretty hard concept to sacrifice Here And Now for something you'll probably never see or experience."

"True enough. To the Tomorrow Is Coming people a tipping point is a moment before an unalterable environmental disaster, for the Here And Now people the tipping point is the moment beer begins to pour out of the glass into the throat." McLeish chuckled at his own humor. "Yeah, well tomorrow is coming pretty damn quick for some people. Take the Chumash, for instance. Their people have been living and traveling through that gorge area for thousands of years. There are archaeological sites everywhere. The pipeline company plans to dig a hundred-yard wide swath to lay their new pipe. That's a whole lot of culture that could be torn up or buried forever." He glanced at Zack. "There's another motive to tuck away in your thinking."

"Figures!" Zack said. "I knew Indians would be involved somehow."

CHAPTER SEVEN

After devouring a delicious Tan Ferrari cordial for dessert, Zack was more than ready for sleep. He stood, put on his hat and pulled out his wallet. "I'll pick this one up," he said. "We've got our own budget line."

McLeish stood, raised an eyebrow. "Must be nice."

Zack paid and they walked out into the chill of the early spring evening. In the parking lot, they paused to finalize their plans.

"I booked a room for you, I hope you don't mind," McLeish said. "It's close, in the Marriott. Go west here, turn right at the filling station. It's a quarter mile on the left. Can't miss it. Nice place. They've even got a Starbucks in the lobby." His eyes narrowed. "What are your plans tomorrow?"

"Not set. I need a lot of information. I'll likely take another look at the gap. We haven't talked about the fiery ghost dancer motorists reported. I want to see how that was done. Also, look for sign from whoever took that shot at Halligon."

McLeish eyed him. "I heard you're quite the tracker."

"I've got help coming if I need it. Give me a call when you learn anything, yeah?"

They shook hands and McLeish drove home to his family while Zack found his way to the Marriott. His room was more of a suite with a fold-out couch. He grunted in satisfaction at that. You never knew when Eagle Feather might appear.

A thousand thoughts buzzed in his head about the current case, but he knew better than to let them take over. Tomorrow was another day. He called Libby and Bernie to say goodnight, flipped off the light and went to sleep.

The following morning the sun streamed in the window. Zack threw on jeans and a sweatshirt and headed down to the lobby and the Starbucks counter. He returned with a steaming cup of Kenya in his hand and sat on the little balcony, enjoying the sun while the world woke up around him.

He didn't expect to hear anything from McLeish for a while yet and he wanted to get to the trails before too many hikers trampled the area, so after Zack finished his coffee he grabbed a bagel from the courtesy breakfast buffet and drove back down the freeway headed south. He got off at the CA Route 1 intersection and drove down the same access road to the parking area.

Zack felt a chill. It was still cold in the canyon where the mountain rampart screened the sun on this eastern side. He put his pistol in the belt holster and swung it back out of sight, covering everything with the sweatshirt. Zack set off up the trail at a brisk pace and soon was warm.

The trail divide appeared in what seemed a short quarter mile. He took the Trespass Trail and then turned onto the Tunnel View trail, following a sketch he'd made from the trail map. The plank bridges across the first two narrow ravines kept his feet dry, but it was hard to avoid the sticky mud at awkward places and soon his sneakers were slimed. On the other hand, those places offered a story of who or what had passed here before him this morning. He saw there had been a large coyote and a feral pig. There were lots of boot tracks, all too old for his purposes. He came to another trail divide, the Underpass Trail. According to his map, this trail dropped down the slope and eventually passed under the freeway.

Zack took a sip from his water bottle and studied the far canyon wall. It sloped gently up from the highway but steepened rapidly after a quarter mile or so. He thought he could see where the Ortega Trail ran parallel to the highway below it, where they had been yesterday. From where he stood now, it was a long rifle shot. An expert shot. He decided to descend the trail to see if there was a better vantage point.

The trail took him among hummocks and random sandstone boulders. Some appeared random, others almost as if positioned. There was an ancient, unearthly feel to the place, something Zack had felt before in very old forests with hidden secrets. Here it was open meadowland on a hillside with occasional copses of twisted old oaks. Something about the place put him on edge, however, kept him wary.

He would not have seen the footprint otherwise. It wasn't on the mud of the trail but off to the side, more of a tamped down trace in the grass. Zack backtracked to see if he'd missed any others, but there were none. Moving forward he found more, just a slight bending of grasses. The traces edged away from the trail into the thickness of the meadow beyond. Following, his pant legs were soon soaked. He came to a large boulder with a smooth, level top. On its up-slope side, the vegetation was crushed like a deer bed, but the matted grass was mashed deep into the underlying mud. Zack knelt behind the boulder, felt his knees fit into existing impressions and sighted along the top of the rock surface. He gaged the distance to the far slope where the trail traversed to be about four hundred yards, not such a difficult shot for a proficient hunter. Yet the shooter had missed. Maybe the miss was intentional. A warning?

Apparently, the local investigators had not found this location, if they had searched down this way at all. He'd seen no sign of anyone else along the path in the past twenty-four hours. If the shell was ejected into these tall grasses it might still be here somewhere, assuming the shooter had left it. He began a minute search down in the grass.

"Are you looking for this, White Man?"

Startled, Zack brought his head up so abruptly the sloping ground caused him to sit back on his butt.

Eagle Feather's expression did not change. He held up a cylindrical object between thumb and forefinger. It was a brass shell casing.

Zack stared at his friend. Eagle Feather was sitting on a nearby boulder in leather-clad pants wearing a black shirt and brown deerskin vest, looking as if he'd been there all morning. The man had the ability to appear and disappear like vapor. How had he found him here? One thing for sure—Zack wasn't going to ask and give his friend the satisfaction of offering some vague, mystic-sounding response.

"What size shell is it?"

Eagle Feather tilted back the rim of his black reservation hat with the single scrawny feather and peered closely at the inscription.

"It says here 308 W-I-N."

"Ah, three-oh-eight Winchester. That figures. Cheap, hard-hitting, a perfect load for this distance."

"It will kill most animals, maybe not a bear, though. It will kill you."

Zack stood, wiped the mud from his knees. "I don't think it was me he was after. But the shooter expected a long shot. He probably carried a Remington model 700 or a Ruger Precision Rifle or something of that sort." He grinned at Eagle Feather. "Good to see you, friend."

Eagle Feather nodded.

"Tell me, where were you when I called the other day. You kept our conversation rather brief. You weren't in Utah seeing a certain young lady, were you?"

Eagle Feather stared at him for a moment. "They called this a hunting accident."

Zack grinned, then pointed across the valley. "It wasn't an accident. There are very few places where you can make that shot and this is one of them. He was trying to hit—or scare—one of us." He squinted at Eagle Feather. "How did you know about the shooting?"

Eagle Feather's eyes had followed Zack's finger when he pointed. Now he turned with a slight smile. "I drove in early this morning. I listened to the local news. They mentioned a hunting accident, a pipeline security man and two FBI agents so I came right here hoping all the prints hadn't been trampled yet."

Zack gestured toward the trail. "You didn't come this way."

Another hint of a smile. "The shooter did not either. He came along the upper trail from the opposite direction and went back the same way."

Zack raised his eyebrows in surprise. "From the mountain ridge? But I found his sign over there near the trail I came down."

Eagle Feather nodded. "He walked back and forth looking for his best shot."

Zack scratched his cheek and thought about it "The mountain ridge is a long way around yet he got here at the right time."

"Maybe he had information. Maybe he took the opportunity when it offered itself. Maybe it was an accident."

"That pipeline security fellow was the only one who could have been on any kind of schedule."

Eagle Feather shrugged.

"Where's your stuff?" Zack asked.

"In the truck."

"I've got space for you where I'm staying."

"I have a place. It is a place where I can listen and learn." Eagle Feather led back to the trail. He paused, waved an arm around. "Do you feel anything in this place, White Man?"

Zack paused, gave a slow nod. "Yeah. There's something about these old boulders, these groves of ancient oaks."

Eagle Feather regarded him. "I too feel the presence of spirits. Something happened here, something with many people a long time ago." He stood for a moment, head tilted slightly, then moved on.

They stopped on the packed dirt of the main trail.

"Where's your truck?" Zack asked.

Eagle Feather nodded toward the freeway. "I parked off the ramp at the interchange. I did not have much information from the news. I had to find my way."

Zack glanced at his watch. He pointed across the valley. "There's history over there you need to know. Also a thing or two about a pipeline. What say you go get your truck and we meet in Buellton at the McDonalds."

"That sounds good. I could eat a horse." He paused. "I would not, though."

Once they'd received their order and found a corner table at the nearly empty McDonalds, it took just fifteen minutes for Zack to sum up everything he'd learned since he'd arrived the day before. Eagle Feather ate his breakfast and listened.

"You said Agent McLeish is visiting crematoriums this morning?" he said, finally, when Zack had finished.

Zack nodded.

"Are there no other sources for such a fire?" Eagle Feather asked.

"I think McLeish will be asking that question."

Eagle Feather tilted his head. "What happens if a rifle bullet penetrates a high-pressure oil pipeline?"

Zack raised his eyebrows. "That is a very good question." He studied Eagle Feather. "Are you thinking this guy might have that in mind?"

"I think a man who is willing to shoot at an oil man would be willing to shoot a pipeline."

Zack picked up his phone. "I'll give McLeish a call, see what he's learned. Then I'll talk to Halligon. He might know the answer to your question." He glanced at Eagle Feather as he punched in the first number. "What are your plans?"

"I will go to see my host. After that, I have some questions for people who know things."

CHAPTER EIGHT

McLeish picked up the phone at the first ring. Zack heard murmuring sounds in the background, drifts of quiet conversation which echoed as if in a hollow place.

McLeish was whispering. "Hi, Zack. You'll never guess where I am. Never mind, I won't make you. I'm in a crematorium at the Lorenzo & Sons Funeral Home in Santa Maria. Listen, there are eight crematoriums in the immediate Santa Barbara vicinity and there are two in Santa Maria but none in between. Does that say something about life expectancy in those places, I wonder?"

"I'm sure the good citizens of Santa Ynez Valley don't want that kind of smoke floating over their area."

"You are probably right. But bottom line, it means the killer or killers had to transport basically a bag of bones over thirty miles, one way or the other."

"And then somehow carry the remains a mile or more along the trail, climb that knoll with it and set it afire again. That's a lot of trouble to make a point, whatever it is."

He heard McLeish grunt. "Beyond that, from what Mr. Lorenzo here tells me, they have very strict protocols regarding the cremation process. You must be trained and certified to touch the unit, every step is logged and verified, records are kept minute by minute. You can't just take this thing for a Saturday afternoon cruise."

"How many have you visited?"

"Just the two here in Santa Maria. But the directors tell me I can expect procedures just as tight in all the Santa Barbara area crematoriums—if not tighter."

"No bribes, that kind of thing? What do the local gangsters do with bodies?"

McLeish chuckled. "They don't come to these places. For one thing, there is no vacancy for weeks. Lorenzo tells me they have to get the job done within a certain timeframe, mandated by the state. With a minimum of three hours to complete cremation and even longer for beefier people, he says it's all they can do to stay within the state timeframe." His voice dropped to more of a whisper. "Lorenzo told me about this shady deal in Paramus, New Jersey where bodies stacked up like logs at a lumber mill for months. He says it can't happen here in sunny California."

"So we look elsewhere?"

"If I knew where to look. I'm expecting more today from forensics regarding the fuel used to burn the body. That should give us a direction." He paused. "What have you been up to?"

Zack gave McLeish a quick rundown of his morning, including meeting Eagle Feather, locating the site used by the sniper and the man's escape over the mountain ridge.

"No wonder we couldn't trap him. Must be a local, though, to know those trails."

"All the issues we've suggested for motive are local," Zack pointed out.

"True."

"We found his shell casing, a .308 Winchester. That suggests certain rifles. Why don't you have a man check retailers, gun clubs, and the like to see who owns one."

McLeish grunted. "You're talking about maybe the world's most popular big game load."

"Yeah, yeah, I know. But let's just see where that puts us. I've got the shell casing bagged. I left it in my room in the safe. I've left a room key and a key to the safe for you with the desk clerk. Maybe we'll get lucky and find a fingerprint."

"I'll get it."

"I've got some other lines to investigate. Eagle Feather has his own direction. How about we all meet tonight here at the Marriott, say five?"

"See you then."

Zack tried Halligon's number but got no answer. He did a computer search for a local gun shop and drove to the Maxi-Tact Gun Shop in Santa Maria. As he entered the store he heard the pop-pop of firing from an indoor range. Shelves were lined with a variety of automatic guns. Rarely seen weaponry from bazookas to light machine guns were on display. Zack approached a salesperson and explained his purpose.

"You're looking for a rifle that can penetrate a high-pressure oil pipeline? We won't assist you with anything illegal here."

Zack showed his FBI credentials. "You wouldn't mind helping prevent something illegal, then?"

"Absolutely not."

"Well, my first question is, can a .308 Winchester do the job?"

The man, tall with beefy arms protruding from his short sleeve T-shirt, pulled at his wiry black beard. "Not likely, from what I know of the steel wrapping they use on those things. Maybe a self-loaded mag could do it. But I think you're looking at a .338 mag for that job. You'd need that kind of punch." He called over to a second salesperson. "Hey, Ike, what was that story you told me about the guy shooting the pipeline in Alaska?"

Ike lumbered over. He was shorter than the first man but beefier with red hair clipped close and freckles on his arms. He was grinning as he approached.

"Yeah, that was back in 2001. The guy was drunk, had a .338 magnum he fired from a Winchester Savage 110. He never thought it would penetrate, but he hit the pipe near a valve, maybe a weak spot. They found the rifle, then nailed the guy cause he had blood on his face and a black eye from the scope, like a big sign saying, "I did it!" Ike laughed. "Those .338 mags are not comfortable. They kick like a mule."

"Anyway, by the time the authorities got there the jet of oil from the pipe had bent it into a curve and sprayed a quarter mile into the trees. The force of the spray at the pipe would have taken your hand off. The oil spewed out for days before they got it turned off.

They lost 285,000 gallons of crude and the cleanup cost thirteen million." Ike looked at Zack. "What's the question?"

The other salesman spoke for him. "Man wants to know if a .308 WIN could penetrate the pipe."

Ike shook his burly head. "Naw, never happen. But he could probably chamber a .338 WIN in the same rifle. Winchester has the only bullet that size would fit." Ike chewed slowly on something, studying Zack. "Now understand, that Alaska pipeline penetration was a lucky shot. Had to be from just the right distance, not too close, not too far, and dead on square. And like I said, that was in 2001. By now they got pipe a bazooka would have trouble penetrating."

"So no, can't be done," Zack said.

Ike put both hands in the air. "Not sayin' that. You got a whole lot of depends goin' on here. Never say never."

"I guess the .308 WIN is a pretty common load?" Zack asked.

Ike guffawed. "The Winchester hunting rifle line loaded with the .308 is like looking for a Chevy Coupe in the sixties—they are everywhere you look. My grandmother's got one." He paused, a funny look came on his face. "Actually, my grandmother does have one."

By the time Zack left the shop, he had a pocket full of brochures and six free tickets for the range. Just as he climbed into the Jeep his phone rang.

"Zack, it's James McLeish. Just got the info from forensics. Their analysis of the fuel used to burn the victim shows ninety-five percent paraffin and five percent carbon black."

"Paraffin? You mean kerosene?"

"Yeah. Unusual, apparently. Crematoriums use LPG or fuel oil."

"Doesn't kerosene burn hotter?"

"Too hot for crematoriums, I'm told. It can cause problems with the equipment."

"What's carbon black?"

There was a pause. "Well, I'm guessing the carbon is the residue from the incomplete combustion of the body."

"Makes sense. So what now?"

"Now all I gotta do is figure out where else the body could have been burnt with those fuels. I'll see you at five." McLeish rang off.

Zack glanced at his watch. He had another three hours before the meeting. His thoughts went to the history of the Corliss woman and her ironic and very unfortunate fate. There was no doubt in his mind the killer had known this history and expected others to know it. How common was this knowledge, actually? He decided a late afternoon coffee and a session with his computer might be a good idea.

He walked down the corridor to his room with a steaming cup of Starbucks coffee in his hand. He nearly spilled it trying to operate the key scan. He nearly dropped it when he saw the interior of his room. His belongings were everywhere; clothing was strewn about, the couch cushions on the floor, drawers half open. His computer lid was up and the FBI protective screen told him an attempt had been made to hack into it. He walked to the closet and looked at the safe. The door was still locked and scratches around the handle and edges suggested someone made a crude attempt to gain access. *I'm not dealing with a master criminal here*, he thought to himself. He opened the safe with his own key. Nothing inside had been touched.

The intruder must have been looking for the shell casing. Zack had nothing else of value to anybody. Two thoughts immediately occurred to him; the shooter must believe there were fingerprints on the shell casing and whoever had searched his room must have seen Eagle Feather when he found it and handed it to him.

Zack didn't bother to report the intrusion to local police. Amateurish as the searcher was, he would have worn gloves. Everyone watches television.

Zack restored the room to order and went for a chat with the desk clerk. The clerk had not seen or heard anything suspicious nor had anyone asked for his room number. He went back to his room and settled into the desk chair to continue his research.

The Corliss story was not easy to find. It was not in any of the Gaviota State Park material, although the Las Cruces Adobe was highlighted. Zack had to dig a lot deeper to uncover the story. The account he finally found matched the one told him by McLeish.

Curious, Zack went back to the lobby and spoke to the desk clerk again. The young woman had spent her entire life in the Santa Ynez Valley but had never heard of the Corliss murder. Zack thanked her. Clearly, the story was not common knowledge. But the inferences from the placement of the burned body and the addition of the hoops were clear. It was aimed at someone who knew the history, perhaps someone who was somehow involved.

Back in his room, Zack located the Lompoc Historical Society, found a number and called. The person who answered was knowledgeable. She had indeed known about the murders and could contribute details.

"You won't find many others who know about it," she said. "It just isn't general knowledge and is of interest only to family descendants, I suppose."

"Was there a particular controversy, beyond the fact the murder went unsolved, that could still be gnawing at someone?"

There was a pause. "Well, I think the question of land ownership might still bother some people. There were several lawsuits around the inheritance of the Corliss property. The posse that performed the initial investigation concluded Mr. Corliss had died first, thus the inheritance of the land would go to the child of Mrs. Corliss by a prior marriage. Yet there is no record of either having a prior marriage, let alone a child from one. Beyond that, the law as interpreted by both the original court case and the 1888 Supreme Court appeal saw their deaths as similar to circumstances of a shipwreck; the loss of all aboard is considered simultaneous regardless of who actually died first or last."

"What was the case about?"

"A Corliss descendant trying to establish title to the ninth part of the property originally purchased by George Corliss."

"What was the outcome?"

"The Hollister estate successfully sued to prevent the division of the Las Cruces Rancho by individual claimants."

"This decision might have left some groups unhappy?"

"No doubt."

"Unhappy enough to kill one hundred thirty years later?"

"I sincerely doubt it."

After the call ended, Zack sat for a long while with steepled hands against furrowed brow thinking. The thing was, there were too many motives, but none seemed strong enough for such an atrocious murder. He found the hotel pad and pen and began to list them.

#*Private land and property issues. Unlikely. Particularly as it is now all owned by the state.*

#*New oil pipeline. This topic crossed several thresholds. Chumash archaeological and cultural sites, environmentalists and water conservation, agriculture, etc. A mishmash of concerns. Possible to likely. But which?*

#*Vengeful act in response to a 130-year-old unsolved murder. Unlikely.*

#*Private, personal concern dressed to look like something else. Possible to likely.*

Zack stared at what he had written. He could not eliminate any motive without more evidence. He sighed and pushed the pad away.

His phone rang. "Zack, Spud here. I'm just checking to see how you're getting on."

"You interested in my comfort and welfare, or the case?"

There was a chuckle. "Both, of course, but I mostly wondered about the case."

Zack let out a groan. "To be honest, not well. There isn't much to go one yet."

"Have you identified the victim?"

"No. That's the biggest obstacle at present. Our hope is that forensics will come up with a DNA match, but it hasn't happened yet."

"Aw, too bad. Did you find anything else at the scene to help?"

"Actually, a funny thing. What we thought were...hang on a moment, someone's at the door." Zack put Spud on hold and went to answer the knock. McLeish stood there. Zack looked at his watch, motioned him in, reconnected with Spud.

"Spud, look, I've got a meeting right now. Let's catch up, maybe do coffee."

"Sounds good, Zack. Later."

Zack went to the safe and removed the shell casing. He handed it to McLeish. "With a bit of luck, we'll find a fingerprint on this. Now if we go down to the lobby, we may find Eagle Feather waiting there."

CHAPTER NINE

There was no Navajo in the lobby. It was early yet, by ten minutes. Zack motioned McLeish to seats in a corner away from the flow of guests. They sat. The grind of the Starbucks coffee mill came to him along with murmured conversation from that corner of the lobby.

Zack smiled. "Eagle Feather will be along shortly. He's got this bad habit of being punctual."

"Shall I begin?" McLeish asked.

Zack nodded. "Sure."

McLeish crossed his legs. "As I told you over the phone, a crematorium is an unlikely option for our killer." He ticked the points off on his fingers. "One, they are tightly governed and supervised. Two, they all use a different fuel, either LPG or fuel oil. Not paraffin. Three, the steel hoops must have been placed on the body at some point just before or during the burning, difficult to do in the crematoriums."

Zack nodded. "So, as you suggested earlier, we are looking for a different location for the burning and perhaps the murder as well."

"Exactly. So I inquired a little deeper into the use of paraffin as a fuel. Most furnaces here in the U.S. use heating oil or gas. Turns out, most of Britain uses kerosene as a heating fuel for homes and businesses." He chuckled. "Incidentally, I also learned paraffin is used by fire dancers, fire breathers, and fire jugglers because of the low flame temperature. Anyway—"

"Whoa, wait a minute. Didn't you tell me earlier crematoriums don't use paraffin because of its *high* heat?"

"Well, yes. That too." McLeish sighed. "Apparently this is a complicated chemistry question, still being studied. As I understand it, cool flame burns around four hundred degrees Fahrenheit. When you consider an ordinary candle burns around fourteen hundred degrees Fahrenheit, you see the difference. But, cool flame can ignite to hot flame in the right chemical circumstance. Or vice versa. A hot flame may appear to be out, but it may actually become a cool flame still burning yet invisible and ready to reignite to hot flame. Add the right chemical stimulant, such as carbon from a burning body, and suddenly you have a hot flame, possibly a very hot flame. That makes the use of paraffin too unstable for crematoriums."

"Jesus!" Zack said. "You lost me at fire jugglers."

McLeish grinned. 'I lost myself in there somewhere. Point is a limited number of homes and businesses in the U.S. currently using kerosene. It's cheaper and burns cleaner."

"But the chemical re-ignition problem?"

McLeish shrugged. "I'd guess the furnaces are specifically designed to screen out foreign matter and probably have to be cleaned on a regular basis."

"So how could somebody introduce a body?"

"Yes, that's the core of the matter." McLeish gave a sudden smile. "The good news is, because kerosene furnaces are rare around here, they shouldn't be too hard to track down, so that's my next project."

Zack leaned closer to McLeish to speak softly. "Speaking of projects, guard that shell casing carefully. Someone turned my room upside down this afternoon looking for it."

McLeish's eyebrows rose in surprise. "Somebody broke in?"

"Yeah, someone must have got hold of a key. Pretty well trashed the place. The desk clerk knew nothing. I—"

His phone buzzed in his pocket. He held up a palm. "Hang on. This might be Eagle Feather."

It was.

"White Man, I need you to come with me."

As accustomed as he was to his friend's quirks, Zack was surprised. "Go where? Where are you?"

"I am in Santa Ynez and I am about to drive to Las Cruces. I need you to meet me at the Gaviota State Park access road next to the ramp on the east side of the freeway. Park your vehicle along the fence there. Bring your hiking shoes. I will find you." He was gone.

Zack looked at McLeish and gave him a wry smile. "I guess our meeting is over. That was Eagle Feather. I'm to meet him."

"What's up?"

Zack shrugged and stood. "I've no idea, but it sounded urgent, meaning he used even fewer words. Let's meet up for breakfast. We need to finish this conversation. You know a good place?"

"Sure, the best! Ellen's Danish Pancake House. I'll leave directions on your phone. Nine o'clock do for you?"

Zack nodded. They shook hands.

Zack ran up to his room, put on a pair of training shoes, grabbed a jacket, and left the hotel. Soon he was on the freeway headed south toward Las Cruces.

He took the off-ramp at the route one intersection and turned left, then right on the access road and pulled up next to the chain-link fence as instructed. His watch said five-thirty, but it was nearly dark. There was no light visible beyond his car, below him a string of headlights headed north on the freeway.

A rap sounded on the passenger side of the Jeep and Eagle Feather slid into the seat.

"Hello, White Man."

Zack nodded. "Hello yourself. What's the big mystery?"

Eagle Feather shook his head. "No big mystery. We are going hunting."

"Hunting what, if I may ask?"

"Big game. You should bring your pistol. I hope we won't need it, though."

With that, Eagle Feather slipped out and closed the door. Zack locked the Jeep and followed him. They moved down the access road toward the parking area at a brisk walk.

"Why didn't we just park down here?" Zack asked when they arrived. The lot was empty. The park officially closed at sundown.

"We don't want our vehicles to be noticed. My truck is parked out of sight."

Eagle Feather led the way up the trail Zack had taken once before. The climb was steep and in the shadow of trees and with the steep embankment it grew progressively harder to see where to place his feet. They took the right fork onto the Trespass Trail, just as Zack had done. This time they bypassed the Tunnel View Trail and continued steeply uphill. The terrain here was open and Eagle Feather moved swiftly. He didn't pause until they were once again in the shelter of trees where the trail swung south on a traverse. They paused to catch a breath.

"When are you going to tell me what this is all about?" Zack asked.

Eagle Feather appeared to be grinning, but Zack couldn't tell for sure.

"I am staying in a place where I can learn things. I believe there will be an event here tonight after dark."

"What kind of an event?"

'You will see when it happens. But first, we must climb high enough to view it from above."

Zack knew he would learn nothing more and gestured for Eagle Feather to lead on. The path was a dirt fire road, rough in places but wide and not too difficult to
negotiate in the darkening shadows. It continued to climb, turned the face of a ridge and led them along the mountainside away from the main Gaviota Gap before turning back westward along the opposite wall. At its face, they came to a vantage point high above the streaming lights of the freeway traffic. Zack could see where the northbound cars exited the tunnel and swept around a curve toward the northwest. Headlights of the southbound traffic moved the opposite way. The slope on the far side of the freeway was now in darkness. High above, the mountain summit ridge drew a black line along the fading sky. Already several stars twinkled above it.

"Now we wait," Eagle Feather said in a low tone. "But no noise."

They each found a comfortable boulder to sit upon. As minutes stretched to a quarter hour and then a half hour the chill settled into Zack's bones. He zipped his jacket snug, clamped his felt hat tight onto his head, and put on the light gloves that were in the jacket pocket. The sky above the western ridge darkened. More stars appeared as bright pinpoints in ever-increasing numbers. The sage, rosemary and coyote brush along the trail near them lost form until only the sweet smell of the rosemary gave evidence it was still there.

Eagle Feather's dark outline was visible when Zack glanced that way. His figure was still. Another ten or fifteen minutes went by. The cold increased. Zack glanced again at Eagle Feather. This time, he was gone.

Then came a grip on Zack's arm, a whisper in his ear. "Come."

Zack let himself be led silently back down the trail into the darker shadow of an oak tree. Eagle Feather pulled him slightly behind the tree, his mouth to Zack's ear. "Quiet now."

They waited. Zack heard a clink, the sound of a small stone being dislodged. He held his breath. Moments later a shadow swept by them on the trail. There was no sound, just the sense of movement.

Eagle Feather maintained his grip on Zack's arm and they remained as they were for several long minutes. Then the grips relaxed, the mouth at Zack's ear whispered, "I did not expect them to come this way. I do not think they saw us."

"Who are they?" Zack asked, in the same quiet tone.

"We must wait to see."

The men moved back to their rocks and sat again. They didn't wait very long this time.

Zack caught his breath in surprise. Across the gorge from them, across the highway low on the opposite slope came a flicker of fire. The fire grew, the flames licked higher, the blaze grew wider. Then in the center a figure formed and began to move, arms and legs gyrating in a kind of slow strange dance. The sight was far from them yet incredibly clear. Headlights of cars slowed as they approached the curve, no doubt entranced by the sight.

61

"What the..." Zack said under his breath.

"Quick, now. Follow me." Eagle Feather was moving back down the trail.

It was near impossible to see underfoot in the tree cover, and Zack caught stones with his toe and nearly pitched forward on to his face several times. Eagle Feather moved ahead without hesitation as if darkness did not exist. Once out of the tree's mantle, the stars and a rising moon lit the path. Eagle Feather moved more swiftly here, kept to the high bank side of the roadway out of sight. At the Tunnel View Trail intersection, Eagle Feather turned in. At once the shadows claimed them and Zack stumbled along. They crossed a wooden bridge, ascended out of an arroyo and dipped into another with a second bridge, and climbed again. Zack's trainers were soaked from puddles he never saw and he was more chilled, despite moving. Still, they kept on. Occasionally Zack had clear views off to his right of the fiery dancing figure.

They came to the Underpass Trail intersection, or at least Zack assumed it was for Eagle Feather turned down the slope. The footing was firm with moist dirt underfoot. They could advance noiselessly. They descended to a bend in the trail where it angled south. Eagle Feather stopped, crouched down. Zack copied him.

Ahead across the meadow, he saw shadows, slight movements, something bright glowing.

Eagle Feather turned to Zack. "You should have your pistol out."

Then he stood and advanced toward the shadowy forms. "Do not move." His voice was loud, commanding. "We are armed and will shoot if you attempt to escape."

CHAPTER TEN

The figures turned on the narrow trail, one standing, the other kneeling, both staring out from under sweatshirt hoods, their faces pale against the background. The kneeling person held something that glowed red.

"Put your hands up where we can see them," Zack said. "You, put that thing down."

They did as they were told. The object on the trail caused a red glow in the tall grass. Zack played his flashlight beam on each person. The faces under the hoodies looked young.

"What are you doing?" Zack asked.

"Nothing," one said. It was the voice of a young girl.

"What is that thing?"

"It's a laser image projector," said the other person in a young male voice.

"You were projecting an image of a dancing person encased in flame," Eagle Feather said.

The two young people nodded.

Zack reached down and carefully picked up the projector. Its shape resembled that of an old video camera, bulky and thick bodied narrowing at the lens. He aimed it into the darkness over the freeway. He saw nothing.

"How does this work?"

The boy spoke, eager to be helpful now. "You must project it onto a reflective surface, like a screen or water."

"What did you project it on?"

The girl spoke. "There is a chalky white cliff face over there. It works on that. Can we put our hands down now?"

"Not just yet. I'm going to pat you down for weapons." Zack handed the projector to Eagle Feather and did a quick pat down on each of them but found nothing. "How old are you?"

They were both seventeen, it turned out. They attended the Santa Ynez High School. Both were Chumash, lived on the reservation.

"Would you like me to show you how it works?" the boy asked.

Eagle Feather handed him the projector.

The boy knelt with it. "It requires a steady hand at this distance because the image jumps with every movement. I need to find the cliff...there it is."

At that moment the flaming figure suddenly appeared across the valley, dancing as if in pain, flames licking around it. It looked very real.

"It uses two monochromatic pure colors, orange and red, and it is collimated, that is it won't spread out over distance nor lose intensity."

"It's like what people use at Christmas to project on their houses," the girl explained.

"Except much more powerful," the boy said. "We are projecting two images, one of flame, the other the figure with a foot raised. We oscillate between the images and the figure appears to dance while the flames flicker."

"Very impressive," Zack said. "Now turn it off and tell me why you are doing this."

"The oil pipeline is threatening our sacred sites," the girl said. "They want to carve a half-mile swath through the valley that will scatter the bones of our people and disturb their rest."

"Not to speak of ruining numerous archeological sites so that nothing can be learned from them in the future," the boy added.

"You think the specter of fire near the pipeline will cause people to think about consequences from building such a pipeline." Zack's voice held a touch of humor.

"Yes, sir."

"Who else is involved? That must be a very expensive instrument."

"No one, sir," the girl said. "Chance and I are working on a physics project together and the science department lent us the laser projector for our work."

"Well, this part of your experiment is over." Zack took their names, wrote them in his little notebook. "How did you get here?"

"We drove here this afternoon, left our car in the carpool area near the highway and hiked up to the rocks"— the girl waved toward the darkness above them—"then snuck down here after dark." She looked down at her feet as if ashamed. "We've done it many times before."

Eagle Feather grunted. "So we have heard."

"Okay, listen closely. I am an FBI agent and you are now in my custody. I want you to go to your car and drive to the McDonalds in Buellton, find a table, and we will meet you there."

As they watched the two figures disappear into the darkness along the path, Zack chuckled. "I can't see either of them shooting a rifle instead of a laser."

"I cannot see them killing a person either," Eagle Feather said. "But they may have seen something if they came here often."

"Those were my thoughts. We can question them at the McDonalds." Zack noticed how his voice seemed to echo in the darkness. A mist had appeared, unnoticed. It had grown colder. He gave a slight shiver. "Time to go."

"Wait." Eagle Feather lay a hand on his arm. "Do you feel it?" His voice was soft but vibrant.

Zack stood still, looked and listened. He did feel something. He glanced above them at the sloping hillside. It was all tall grass, a large meadow with boulders protruding that glowed in the moonlight. The boulders were rounded at the top and cupped as if intentionally carved to hold water. Zack knew it was the effect of soft sandstone weathering away over the eons, but the sight was eerie. He had not noticed before how regular the spacing was between the boulders, rather like...well, tombstones.

"Wait," Eagle Feather whispered. His hand remained on Zack's arm.

The mist climbing up the slope had passed them in tendrils and wisps and appeared to wrap itself around the stones, one by one, then climb them like a rising sea, building above each boulder while leaving a pool of cottony mist between them. The effect was that of watching a sculptor build a statue from the ground up.

Zack could not tear his eyes away. As the fog monoliths grew they took on form and glowed with the luminosity of the moonlight. Zack imagined he could make out details in the forms, a hand here, a face there. It was as if the dead were rising above their graves.

"I knew it," Eagle Feather whispered. "I knew the spirits were here."

They stood and watched the figures take shape, a phalanx of them, all staring across the valley to the far side. The mist continued up the slope, enveloping more boulders, creating more figures. A mist army.

When the moon dipped behind a cloud it broke the spell. The figures disappeared in the darkness, the strange tension in the atmosphere died away.

"It is time to go," Eagle Feather said.

The two men moved swiftly and quietly along the mud path. Neither spoke until they had reached Zack's vehicle.

"My truck is farther up the road out of sight," Eagle Feather said. "I'll see you at the McDonalds." Zack sensed that now was not the time to talk about what they had just seen. The Navajo would speak of it when he was ready.

Twenty minutes later Zack and Eagle Feather were seated at a table in the McDonalds with the two high school students.

"Have you ordered?" Zack asked.

The two young people shook their heads. The boy sat stiffly upright in his chair, very earnest eyes peering from under long black hair. The girl kept her hood on framing light brown hair and almond eyes. Both shook their heads.

"Allow me, then. Burgers and chocolate shakes?"

Both nodded.

Zack went to the electronic board and set up the orders, adding the same for himself and Eagle Feather. When he returned to the table, the young people were chattering away with Eagle Feather.

"The shooter had done the same as you. He or she came from above the trail, from the eastern rim of the canyon, and returned that way," he was saying as Zack sat.

The boy glanced at Zack, spoke to Eagle Feather. "We never saw anyone else. When we heard someone had been killed near the spot where we were projecting, we were afraid to do it anymore. Besides, we thought the woman being burned up would get our message across for us."

"But the news underplayed the murder," the girl said. "There were a few words about a body found there, but that was all."

Zack smiled at them. "We are order number ninety-eight. Should be soon." He glanced at the girl. "How did you know about the body being burnt?"

She looked shyly at him, looked at Lance. "Rumors flew around the school."

"Such as?"

"The biggest rumor was that a woman had been killed, was dragged to a spot near a pipeline and set on fire."

"It was very sketchy," Lance said. "We kept waiting for the newspaper or TV story, but there never really was one. Then the rumors stopped and nothing really changed."

"So you decided to issue a reminder tonight."

They nodded.

Zack glanced up at the board. "Looks like our order is up." He leveled his gaze on the two high school kids. "You've done your job, okay? If the police caught you, you'd be in for a hassle. You seem like nice kids." He stood. "From now on, I want you to use that projector as it was intended when loaned to you. Nothing more, right?"

They both nodded again.

Zack smiled. "Okay, I'm gonna grab some burgers."

After the young people had eaten and gone along their way, Zack and Eagle Feather went to the Firestone Taproom for a beer. It was crowded but they were able to find a table in the corner.

They sat. Zack grinned at Eagle Feather. "One mystery solved, two more to go."

"I do not think those children shot a rifle at anyone," Eagle Feather said.

"I'm inclined to agree. But their fiery protest followed by an actual fiery murder seems a little too coincidental."

"Maybe the murderer took advantage to make it appear they were connected."

Zack thought about it. "You mean the nightly projections gave the murderer the idea?"

Eagle Feather shrugged. "Or just coincidence."

The waitress appeared with their beers. Both men took a long sip. Zack put his glass down, sighed, and looked at Eagle Feather. "How did you know those kids would be out there tonight?"

Eagle Feather almost smiled. "I have a friend on the reservation, someone I met at a pow-wow a few years ago. There are rumors at the high school and there are also rumors on the reservation. These kids don't know a rumor is like a rope—it has two ends."

CHAPTER ELEVEN

Irma Jean worried about her husband. He had grown progressively more distant over the past weeks and months, not from anything she had done as far as she knew. Nor had his feelings toward her seemed to change. It was worse than that, to her mind. He had apparently stopped thinking about her altogether. He was distracted. No, distracted was not strong enough. Obsessed.

The point was in these past months when they were together his mind was elsewhere. His mood was never pleasant, as if something pricked at him continually—a burr in his saddle, her dad would have said. That was bad enough, but in more recent weeks she had seen a shift from general moodiness and discontent to some apparent intense purpose, something that kept him away all hours of the day and night and when he did come home, it was to sit at that damned computer or fall asleep as if drugged. He barely looked at her.

Bill had never been one to share his thinking. That had never bothered her before. He was a solver, an inventor, a creator. To say he thought outside the box was to understate his mental view. In his mind, there was no box. She admired that about him, it was one of the traits that had attracted her to him in the first place. They'd met at Cal Poly where he was a biomedical engineering student and she was a Wine and Viticulture major. He'd literally crashed one of her lectures, simply walked in and begun directing questions at the professor. Most had nothing to do with the day's topic, all seemed oriented toward some private agenda Bill brought with him. The lecturer tolerated this for a time since the questions were stimulating and challenging, but soon he realized Bill was not one of his regular students and began to ask pointed questions in return. When it was apparent Bill did not belong and was on the verge of being removed, he rose with a grin, bowed, and walked out but not before he'd favored her with a wink.

That occurred just months before he was expelled from the school. The administration could not tolerate Bill's particular mode of acquiring an education, which seemed to consist of treating every curriculum offered at the school as his personal smorgasbord and sampling random classes as he saw fit to meet his own objectives. In short, he was creating his own course of study while neglecting the one in which he was enrolled. He may have been the brightest student ever at Cal Poly to receive failures in every single course over three terms before the school completely lost patience.

He did not leave San Luis Obispo empty handed, however. He left with a wife. In the months prior to his termination, Bill had sought out Irma Jean and courted her with the same single-minded approach he'd applied to fulfill his own personal educational objectives. She had no chance. The day Bill was informed of his expulsion they traveled from college to the mission and were married.

Then it was Irma Jean learned the true objective for Bill's short but intense college career. They went shopping. They filled Bill's ancient Land Rover with food supplies, hardware, camping supplies, cooking utensils, and tools. They bought a single axle trailer and loaded it as well. Then they traveled south to Santa Barbara County to ten acres of land Bill had selected where they would live off the grid. Bill's plan gradually became clear to Irma Jean. It was brilliant. Exciting. Inviting, even. Their off-grid life would not be her preconceived notion of an antisocial, bare and harsh existence with a smelly outhouse, limited diet, and no TV. Just the opposite. From her viticulture curriculum she had knowledge for growing vegetables and cultivating olives and grapes and with Bill's chemical, electrical, structural and digital education acquired through his own specific curriculum, not to speak of his natural abilities, they developed a standard of living that surpassed Irma Jean's childhood experience while growing up in her middle-class parents' home in Santa Barbara. Bill's idea of living off the grid did not mean doing without. They had a phone line to connect to the internet with DSL powered by their own solar panels. They had a phone connected through their data line. Bill constructed an ingenious retort furnace and distilling tower to convert pitch to fuel to heat the house and power the stove and water heater.

The turbine and solar panels provided all the remaining energy needed for office, greenhouse, home, and stable. They had farmyard animals and pets. They had a good life.

After Irma Jean's dad died and her mom became unwell they brought her to live with them. They had plenty of room and plenty of food and Irma Jean could nurse her. The care and the company were good for both of them.

Bill's generous and positive mood began to change shortly after the pipeline leak which coated the Gaviota beaches with oil. His reaction didn't surprise her at the time. Both felt a tenderness toward all creatures and to see marine life and sea birds coated in oil was repulsive and shameful. They felt the area would not really be the same for decades after and mourned the fact.

But as the various oil companies, the county, and the state began pushing and pulling among themselves toward a resolution, Bill became increasingly agitated. They watched a plan slowly emerge that involved replacing the current pipeline with a new, smaller one, increasing trucking on the freeway and closing down certain elements of the refining and redistributing plant at Gaviota. Irma Jean had seen all this before. The power that drove oil production would prevail. Past mistakes would be replicated in a more modern way. Life would go on.

As for Bill, it was maddening and moronic. One had to look to the future of the earth's limited resources and transition to safer more reliable ones. To him, building a new pipeline was like building a huge horizontal monolith dedicated to yesterday. It was a promise to continue the predictably disastrous ways of the past. He grew more and more furious, the anger solidifying within him like bile.

One day a man in a pickup truck arrived at their locked gate. He wanted to talk to them about the pipeline plans. The man's name was John Halligon. He was pleasant and reasonable. He brought some very bad news. The pipeline company faced some difficult choices, he explained. They were currently considering two possible routes for the new structure. One route would bring it right through their farm.

"Not if we don't want to sell," Irma Jean said.

Halligon stared at her, then looked at Bill with raised eyebrows. Bill looked down at the table.

Irma Jean realized for the first time that they did not own the property. They were squatters and could be removed with a single swat of the hand, like flies.

After Halligon left, Irma Jean turned on Bill. "Are you telling me you never purchased this property?" Her eyes seemed to redden with rage. "Who owns it, anyway?"

Bill hung his head. "The state owns it," he said. "They were never going to do anything on it, no more than they are doing with that old adobe going to ruin down at the junction." He lifted his head, fire came to his eyes as well. "This land rightly belongs to me. My family owned all of this, it was taken from us illegally. When it reverted to the state, and they did nothing with it, I decided I would. If it wasn't for those damned ruinous oil companies, no one would ever have challenged us." He stood, his chin quivering with his anger.

"But what will become of us? Me, you, my mother?"

Bill calmed himself with the extraordinary self-discipline he demonstrated whenever there was a crisis. It always calmed Irma Jean to see him manage it.

"They have not decided where to run their pipeline yet. They will look for the most cost-effective way." His face seemed frozen with his determination. "I will show them that running it this way is not the best plan." When he went out the door, he took the rifle.

In the days and weeks that followed Irma Jean saw even less of her husband. She knew he was digging somewhere for he would come in with dirty trouser knees. When she asked him what he was doing, he would give a tense grin and say he was building a fallout shelter. "There's bound to be fallout," he would say.

As worried as she was, Irma Jean had other concerns. Her mother was failing. After her dad had passed, her mom refused to see a doctor. Bill's fundamentalist stance tended to support this refusal, although he never actually intervened. Irma Jean suspected cancer.

There was pain, but their plentiful crop of marijuana provided all the CBD needed to alleviate it.

For a time, life seemed to ease. No decision had yet been reached with the pipeline, Bill's mood lightened somewhat, Irma Jean's mother seemed slightly better. But it was not to be.

Halligon returned to inform them the pipeline was coming their way. He seemed sincerely sympathetic. "You've got several weeks, maybe longer before the first dozer gets here. But you're gonna have to move all this." He waved an arm to indicate their entire farm. "They're clearing a half mile either side of the trench. Anything left here when they arrive gets plowed under." He shook his head. "Sorry, folks."

After he left, Bill sat still. Irma Jean had been preparing herself for this eventuality ever since that first meeting. She put a hand on his arm. "Bill, we can start again. We always have my mother's house and property. We can remake our lives."

Bill never moved, never spoke. He sat stiff, face set, staring ahead, seeing nothing. After that, she saw even less of Bill. He was constantly gone, off in the woods somewhere, sometimes into town, sometimes working on some mysterious tasks around the farm. The farm itself was neglected, the animals would have gone unfed and uncared for had Irma Jean not taken over their care. Then Irma Jean's mother turned worse and died.

From that moment it was a horror show for Irma Jean. She wanted a Christian burial for her mother at the church where her father lay buried. Bill refused. He would not expose them to the curious crowds who would gather to see the evicted family. He would not bear the false sympathy of the oil company people and government administrators who would attend out of duty. They began as an independent family, off the grid and they would finish that way.

"But she's my mother!"

"Yes, she deserves better."

"But there is no better! There is no alternative."

Bill assured her there was. They'd bury her right here on the land they developed, near her favorite tree swing—right there.

"But the service?"

"We'll bring in the priest. It will be an intimate private service. Who else that we want would come, anyway?"

Irma Jean's fists clenched, her eyes poured over. "But, Bill, it's not our land!"

Bill's jaw set. "They won't take it. Not when they know someone is buried here."

Irma Jean was so choked up she could hardly speak. "They'll bulldoze her up. I don't want my mother bulldozed up!"

Bill shook his head, his look grim. "No, they won't. That will never happen. I promise you that."

CHAPTER TWELVE

Ellen's Pancake House in Buellton was renown in the area and crowded. The restaurant had a long history of serving its famous Danish pancakes, yet the interior reflected simplicity and efficiency. Quite like a diner, Zack thought, with a breakfast bar the length of the room and tables crowded together like a logjam on a river. Despite the rustic almost primitive ambiance there was always a crowd just outside the door.

McLeish was able to score a table for them in a back room where they had a bit more privacy. He and Eagle Feather met for the first time, each taking the other's measure with a long look. Zack figured the assessment had been mutually favorable from the reactions of both men.

Now McLeish set down his fork. "So, from what you say, the mystery of the dancing fiery figure in the gap is solved."

Zack nodded. "I don't think that particular apparition will bother motorists again any time soon. In a way, though, our job just got harder. If the same culprits had been involved with the image, the murder, and the shot at Halligon, we'd be done now."

"Many factions have a stake in the future of the Las Cruces lands," Eagle Feather said. "Not just the Chumash."

"I agree," McLeish said. "Which means it's possible each crime could have been committed by a separate and distinct person or group."

A despondent quiet fell over the men as they thought about that.

"That's probably how we need to proceed," Zack said. "We can't assume there is a connection. Eagle Feather has his ear to the ground near the Chumash camp." Zack looked at the Navajo. "Why don't you see what you can learn about the sniper who shot at

Halligon. Maybe see if you can backtrack him from the site." He turned to McLeish. "We still need to solve the puzzle of where the body was originally incinerated. What's your plan for that?"

"I plan to contact kerosene distributors in the area to determine who purchases quantities for a large furnace or incinerator and see where that leads me."

Zack nodded. "Sounds good. I'm going to concentrate on the Corliss murder history, who might know it or be expected to know about it or care, and try to figure out how a woman can go missing for this long without anybody noticing." He looked at McLeish. "Some DNA conclusions would sure be helpful."

McLeish nodded, grinned. "Don't worry, Zack, the second I know something I'll call you."

After McLeish departed Zack and Eagle Feather stood together in the parking lot. The morning sun warmed them, a palm tree near the trailer court waved gently. Eagle Feather broke the silence.

"You want to know what we saw last night, don't you, White Man."

"Do you know?" Zack asked.

"I am told a battle was fought there many centuries ago. As long as anyone can remember, there was a Chumash village at the mouth of Gaviota Gap. The people lived off the bounty of the sea. They were a peaceful, contented people. But inland there lived a more warlike tribe, the Tulare Band. Each year they came to the sea for the mussels and abalone shells and to bathe in the sea waters. Often the Chumash would go and hide until the Tulare were gone. Sometimes the Chumash fought and many died. The elders say the place we saw is such a battlefield."

Zack said nothing, staring off at the distant mountain ridge. He turned to look at Eagle Feather. "I felt strongly I should not be in that place."

Eagle Feather nodded. "It was not a good time to be there. The warriors were gathering."

They stood together another minute in silence, then walked to their vehicles.

Zack travelled west from Buellton on Route 246 to Lompoc. Just beyond the traffic circle he pulled over and called the Lompoc Historical Society. No one answered. A message gave him a name and an individual number to try. He did.

"Maple residence."

"Yes, hello. I'm calling for a Miss Maureen Maple?"

"Yes?"

"I tried the Historical Society number and was directed here. I am an FBI agent seeking some background information and hoped you might help."

Zack explained his interest in the Las Cruces and Gaviota Gap area history. He sensed an immediate curiosity on the part of Miss Maple. She invited him to come to her home. He found it easily, a modest single-story affair immaculately kept, a pair of ornamental coconut palms on either side of the walkway.

Miss Maple met him at the door. She was just as he imagined she would look with blue-tinged white hair, lively blue eyes, and a fringed crocheted blouse. Zack followed her to a small sitting room with two comfortable-looking chairs separated by a tea table. The walls were completely lined with bookshelves and a small window desk overflowed with files and notepads.

"Can I offer you something to drink?"

"Just water, if that's okay."

She stepped out and Zack heard the clink of ice in another room. He glanced at book titles. The area directly opposite him seemed dedicated to European History.

She returned and handed Zack a cold glass and a tiny napkin that served only to make holding the glass more complicated. She sat in the other chair, smoothed her skirt, and said, "How may I assist you?"

"I spoke with someone at the Historical Society recently and hoped to follow up on those inquiries. The FBI is investigating a tragic death in the Las Cruces area recently. Perhaps you've heard about it?"

She shook her head. "Not really. I believe I had heard about a body they found there. Something about it being burnt. I didn't pay a lot of attention, these things happen from time to time." She made a gesture of dismissal with a bony hand.

Miss Maple looked prim and delicate as she sat with her hands clasped together on top of her skirt. Zack was struck by how casually she engaged in a topic of such a harsh nature. The smell of lavender and English black tea in the atmosphere made it even more incongruous.

"That is true, ma'am. The body—"

Miss Maple reached out and lay her hand over his. "Do call me Maureen," she said and smiled as she removed it again.

Zack smiled. "Maureen, then. And please call me Zack." He plowed on. "An unusual element of this death is the apparent attempt to use the body to bring attention to a historic murder in the area. You see, hoops were found looped around the body in much the same way hoops from a skirt of the period were found gathered at the neck of the victim found there a hundred and thirty years ago."

"The Corliss murders."

"Yes, that's right." He eyed her. "You don't seem surprised."

She gave a faint smile. "There has been a run on information regarding the Corliss murders over the past month. You are the third person to inquire about it."

Zack felt a rush of interest. "Really!"

She smoothed her skirt over her legs again. "Yes, indeed. Just a few days ago another man from the FBI came into the shop..."

"The shop?"

"Oh, I'm sorry. It is what we who work there call the museum. Anyway, he was very interested in the Corliss tragedy."

"Would that have been agent James McLeish?"

"Yes, I believe that was his name."

"And the other?"

"The other man made his inquiries quite a while earlier, several months, I believe."

Zack tried to keep the tremor from his voice. "Who was that person?"

Maureen put a finger against her chin. "You know, I can't quite come up with his name. He was young, as I recall, and quite athletic in appearance. He came to the shop, just dropped in one day with rather vague questions about the history of the area."

"What area?"

"Well, the Las Cruces land grant and the Gaviota Gap seemed to interest him particularly."

"But you say he inquired about the Corliss affair?"

Her mouth twitched in a slight smile. "Well, I mentioned it, you see, just in passing, but he rather latched onto the subject. It seemed to fascinate him."

"But you can't remember his name."

"No, not off hand. We do have a registry in the shop, but I remember he forgot to sign it. I checked, you see, because I was curious about him. He seemed such an interesting man, well informed, knowledgeable, yet quite, well, authoritative, or perhaps I mean decisive?" Her shrewd eyes studied Zack. "But we seem to have gotten sidetracked. Didn't you have questions about the Las Cruces history?"

Zack nodded. "Yes, that's right. I understand that the Corliss murders may have come about from ill will brought about by competition for the franchise stagecoach stop."

She nodded. "There were several possibilities put forward, but most historians believe that is the most likely motive."

"I learned there was contention over the division of the original Las Cruces land grant as late as 1888. A Corliss family member was involved in a court proceeding. I gather George Corliss had a ninth interest in the property at the time of his death?"

She nodded. "That is so."

"What happened to it?"

"Generally, all the Las Cruces land became absorbed by the Hollister Ranch, one way or another. The Hollister Company sold Rancho Las Cruces to the state in the 1960s."

"So the state of California has owned the property for the last fifty years or more?"

"That's correct."

Zack shook his head in frustration. "That would seem to obviate any motive related to ownership of the land, just as your associate had thought."

"It is hard for me to think of any motive at all related to the Corliss affair that could stir up that sort of feeling today."

Zack shook his head. "Yet the placement of the body, the burning, and the hoops point directly to it."

"A red herring, perhaps."

Zack sighed. "I keep coming back to that." He narrowed his eyes. "Can you tell me anything more about that first man? Was there anything about him—his clothing, a scar, anything at all that stands out for you?"

She sat in silence for a moment. "I suppose the most notable thing about him was his bearing. You know, very straight, upright. And as I said, he seemed quite athletic. He was very direct. There was always eye contact. Self-assured."

"What did he wear?"

"Well, it was winter, of course. He wore a wool sweater, black, I think. And those funny mottled pants they all wear."

"Mottled? Do you mean camouflage? Was he in the military?"

"Well, yes, I shouldn't be surprised. Many of the town's population are involved with the base." She smoothed her skirt.

"Actually, that information is most helpful. It may direct my investigation in a whole new way."

Zack took his leave of Miss Maple after thanking her profusely and requesting she call immediately if anything new occurred to her. Once in the Jeep, he called Spud. When his friend answered, he said, "This is FBI Deputy Assistant Director Zack Tolliver asking AFOSI agent Spud Jarvis for permission to pursue my investigation within Vandenberg Air Force Base."

CHAPTER THIRTEEN

Spud met Zack at the Vandenberg Visitor's Center. As they waited for McLeish to join them, Spud processed an identity card to allow Zack to pass in and out of the base. As a senior agent in the AFOSI (Air Force Office of Special Investigations) at Vandenberg, Spud was able to issue maximum clearances.

"I've got a similar card prepared for Special Agent James McLeish. You two can enter the base twenty-four-seven, but as a courtesy check in with me. Besides, there are certain areas you would still need me to gain access."

Zack nodded. "I'd want your assistance most of the time anyway since I don't know my way around." He glanced at Spud. "What can we do about Eagle Feather? He's part of my team, but he's not strictly speaking a U.S. citizen."

Spud laughed. "Your Indian friend? He's not in any guise a U.S. citizen, strictly speaking, or not. But in some ways, he'll be easier. Get him out here and I'll get him a guest pass as a ranking dignitary from another nation."

Zack grinned. "He's an alien, all right." He saw a car pull up outside the guardhouse window. "That looks like McLeish now."

The two men walked out to the parked car. Zack made the introductions. "Sorry to pull you away so abruptly, James. I've learned there's a good chance our killer may reside on or be connected in some way to the base here. That sheds a whole new light on things."

McLeish scratched his chin. "That sure would. How good is your information?"

Spud interrupted. "Let's not discuss it here, gentlemen. Let's go to my office." He handed McLeish an identity card. "We can take my car."

Spud's office was a short ride from the gate in the Support Group Headquarters building. His office was small but well furnished with comfortable leather chairs and a sofa. His desk and files were at the window. Zack and McLeish sat on the sofa. Spud went to a small refrigerator and extracted three water bottles, tossing one to each of them. He dropped into a chair facing them.

"Now we can talk," he said.

Zack told the agents what he had learned from Miss Maple. He looked at McLeish. "I called you right away because this could fundamentally change your search for the fuel. There might be a need for it here on the base."

"What fuel is that?" Spud asked.

McLeish answered. "The victim was burned with a fuel that is ninety-five percent paraffin and five percent carbon black."

Spud suddenly began laughing.

The other two men stared at him, startled.

"Rocket fuel!" Spud said, still chortling. "You've just described rocket fuel." He waved his arms in an arc. "Yeah, we might have a bit of that around here somewhere." He began to laugh again.

"You use kerosene to fire rockets?" Zack asked.

"Absolutely. It burns cool, but partnered with an element such as carbon black it develops explosive power. It's used particularly for the first stage." Spud was still chuckling.

"I don't know why you are amused," McLeish said. "That leads the trail of the murderer right to your doorstep."

Zack grinned at Spud. "He's right. Particularly when combined with my new evidence that a military type was exploring the history of the Las Cruces region a few months ago."

Spud shook his head. "I will say I'm not delighted your investigation is now centered at the base. But at least I can help." He eyed Zack. "I have a rough idea of what's going on from your descriptions. But to help you, I'll need to be briefed."

The men spent the next hour revisiting everything they'd learned since the case began. Spud was happy to know they could eliminate the fiery dancer from their investigation, but the rifleman who shot at Halligon was another matter.

"Eagle Feather is working on that part," Zack said. "Let's let him continue and see where it takes him. Meanwhile, if our investigation takes us down that road, so much the better."

McLeish turned toward Spud. The leather upholstery groaned slightly under the big man's weight. "We need to know who had access to that particular fuel within the past week or weeks in such a situation the killer or killers could have fired it and burned the woman. I think that is our starting place now."

Spud nodded. "I'm going to do just what you were doing, follow the money. I'll check appropriations to see which groups made the purchase." He cocked an eyebrow. "It could be several, you know."

Zack nodded. "What about the wine barrel hoops? Can anyone bring something like that onto the base and into a facility where they fire such fuels?"

"That's a very good question," Spud said. "Up to a couple of years ago, I'd have said absolutely not. But recently we've been leasing pads and facilities to private organizations using their own rockets. They provide their own security while the base security acts as more of an overall umbrella. Anyone with access to the base can bring in hardware such as that. Residents could be working with wine casks in flower gardens or even fermenting their own brew. It's their business. So if the hoops were in the back of someone's car while they drove to their job, our security wouldn't take notice. As to bringing them into a secure facility leased by a private company, that would be up to their own security."

McLeish shook his head. "It's getting more and more complicated."

Spud sighed. "It sure is. Even my appropriations checks won't be simple since I'll have to request the records of several businesses in addition to all the Air Force budgets."

Zack's eyes opened wide. "That sounds like it could take weeks."

Spud nodded slowly. "I can get help and we can find ways to streamline the process, but it won't happen in an hour."

"Assuming this woman didn't wander under a rocket as it fired, where on base could the fuel be ignited and a body placed in the way?"

"Well, we have several labs where that could be done. The question is, which ones could be available and to whom privately, say, during off hours." Spud drummed his fingers, thinking. "Tell you what, I'm going to get a list of head engineers for projects involving such labs and get those gentlemen to come in for you fellows to interview. We can get that going right away." He turned to his directory, picked up his phone and began calling. He waved at the coffee machine as he did so. "Help yourselves."

After fifteen minutes of drinking coffee and listening to Spud's end of many conversations, the AFOSI agent rattled the phone into its cradle for a final time and stood and stretched with cat-like grace. He walked over and poured himself a coffee and then settled back in an armchair as the others watched like birds hypnotized by a snake.

"Well?" McLeish asked.

Spud gave a weary grin. "Gentlemen, here is what I have learned. On this base currently we have fifteen active rocket pads useful and available for programs, twenty-five silos also useful and available, three underdeveloped silos awaiting funds or other considerations, and five coffin pads stripped of equipment and completely empty. In addition, we have a test pad, TP-01, available for testing rocketry of all types, Complex 395B for testing and training, and Complex 395A that is unused and has been stripped of all equipment. That's all."

Zack and McLeish simply stared. The numbers were staggering, overwhelming.

Spud watched their faces and nodded. "I know, I know. Where to begin?"

"And the active programs?" Zack asked.

"There are several, but all are top secret and no information is available." He smiled wearily. "Even for me."

"The commercial programs?" McLeish asked.

"The fact is, none of the active programs, whether military or commercial, utilize the paraffin and carbon black mixture you describe. None."

Zack shook his head in disbelief. "Where does that leave us then?"

"I see two possibilities," Spud said. He drummed his fingers on his legs as he thought. "First, someone has managed to re-appropriate paraffin and carbon black and set up shop with a spare rocket engine in one of the empty silos or test facilities. Second, someone has access to both the paraffin and the carbon black somehow and is doing his own experiments off-hours in Complex 395B."

"You mean an engineer already assigned to one of the programs ongoing in Complex 395B is readjusting the fuel in his off hours."

Spud nodded.

Zack looked at McLeish first, who shrugged, and then looked back at Spud. "Wouldn't it be rather difficult to lug fuel and a spare rocket engine to one of those empty silos?"

Spud grinned. "I just threw that one out there. Again, it would be a matter of re-appropriating all the equipment and directing it to his silo. But believe me, as one with his finger on security here, it would be very difficult to manage without being discovered."

"Just to commit a single murder," McLeish added.

"That's a good point," Zack said. "We shouldn't put the cart before the horse. I think we are looking for someone who had his own secret experiment already in the works, already set up and ready to go. The decision to commit murder came along after that."

"The murder method was determined by what was available," Spud said.

"Like that," Zack said.

"That leaves us with scenario number two. Let me make another call."

Spud set down his coffee on the side table and went back to his desk. He was on the phone for a long time before he hung up and looked at the two FBI agents.

"Okay, that took a while. There's a lot of secret stuff going on at the testing complex. But the site overseer was finally willing to tell me that they do keep a store of the mix there. He wouldn't tell me how much. I did ask if any has gone missing. He doesn't believe so but will check their logs and call me back."

"With all this secret stuff, how can we know who we need to interview, and for that matter, how can we get clearance to talk to him or her even if we have a suspect?" Zack was feeling frustrated by this whole business.

Spuds face was grim. "That's my bit. It can be tricky, but it's my job." He stood, stretched, looked at his watch. "I'm going to go to the Base Commander and ask her for the names and backgrounds we need. It's past time for lunch. Go on over to the Pacific Coast Club and get some lunch." He grinned, handed Zack a card. "Put it on my tab. I'll meet you there when I've got what we need. You can walk there. Just head on out along California and turn right on Nebraska. You can't miss it."

As they stepped out into the California sunshine, Zack admitted to himself he was enjoying the climate. As much as he loved his own canyon region, it was still cold at night back home and the sun not quite as warm. The walk along the pavement warmed him a little too much and he realized once again he was overdressed.

Zack recognized the club immediately. He led McLeish in and headed for the Cafe, where they were well within the lunchtime. A waiter found a table for them despite the crowd. Spud's ID card seemed to work wonders. As they sipped water and scanned the menu, Zack asked McLeish his thoughts on the way the case had turned.

McLeish looked up from his menu, tilted his head and thought about it.

"I guess I'm not quite one hundred percent sold we're in the right place. Although I have not yet found an incinerator of sufficient size using kerosene somewhere in the region, I don't think it unlikely I could. Also, I'm thinking about the rifleman and remembering he or she knew the trails out there really well. That doesn't sound like Air Force personnel with busy schedules at the base." As Zack started to say something, McLeish put up a hand. "I know, they could be two unrelated circumstances, just as the fiery dancer turned out to be, or at least so we believe."

Zack eyed McLeish. "You still think after meeting those kids one of them could have shot at Halligon?"

"Or us, don't forget. The shot could have been meant for the FBI." He shrugged. "But no, it's hard to believe it could be one of the kids." He looked back down at the menu. "We gotta keep all possibilities alive until proven impossible."

Zack chuckled. "And even then, in my experience—"

"Yeah, I know. Even then."

They each ordered the burger plate, which was the special of the day. Zack had a lager and McLeish had a gin and tonic.

The place had begun to thin out by the time Spud arrived. Zack glanced at his watch. The place stopped serving lunch at 13:30. Spud still had a half hour. He glanced up at him.

"So, how'd it go?"

Spud pulled out a chair, sat, and asked the approaching waiter for the usual. He looked at Zack and grinned. "All set."

"Yeah?"

"The base commander made some calls. We were able to narrow it down to just two real possibilities. The heads of both programs are coming to see us." He looked at his watch. "One at 14:00, the other at 15:00 at my office."

"Perfect," McLeish said. He studied Spud. "You must have some kind of influence here to get this arranged so quick."

Spud gave them a rare serious look. "Security is the number one priority on this base. That's from me and that's from the boss. If we've got someone firing up rocket fuel on their own agenda, we've got a very large security problem. Wasn't hard to get help with this."

On the walk back to Spud's office, Zack put in a call to Eagle Feather.

CHAPTER FOURTEEN

Eagle Feather had to wipe the sweat from his palms to keep his phone from slipping from his hand when he answered the call. A breeze off the ocean mists below felt cool on his moist brow. The blue Pacific Ocean wore a white collar where waves broke along the shoreline, glittered here and there along its great expanse where the reflected sun darted between cloud shadows, and finally faded into the mist in the far distance.

"Hello, White Man."

"Hey, Eagle Feather. Where are you?"

"I am on a ridge overlooking the Pacific Ocean."

"You are tracking the shooter?"

"Yes, I am."

"What have you learned?"

Eagle Feather glanced behind him at the rock face he had just scrambled up and the steep trail on beyond it. "I have learned he is in excellent shape."

There was a pause. "You've seen him?"

"No. I have followed his path."

"Where has it taken you?"

"It has taken me to a place where I can look down on a large oil storage facility. I think it is the oil flow terminus for the off-shore oil platforms I can see from here."

"Interesting. We are at the Air Force base to see which rocket projects use the same solution of paraffin and carbon black used to immolate the victim. We'll be interviewing project managers this afternoon."

"Jets also use paraffin fuel."

"What was that?"

"Do not forget jets also use such fuel. Have you checked at the airfield?"

"How do you know that?"

"I have served my country."

A pause. "You never told me about that."

"There are some things I have not told you, White Man."

"What do you plan to do now?"

Eagle Feather looked down the steep slope before him. "I will follow this man to see where the trail ends."

"Okay. Let's meet for dinner. Think you can make five p.m. at the Firestone Pub?"

Eagle Feather glanced at the sun. "If I cannot, I will phone you."

After the call, Eagle Feather came down from the rock outcrop he'd climbed to get his bearings and continued along the path. The ridge top widened to a meadow of knee-high grass. Here the trail divided. One continued along the ridge, the other appeared to descend down the mountainside. Eagle Feather studied the intersection for a minute or two, then followed the trail leading downward. It was little more than an animal trail but frequented enough to be worn to a dirt surface where footprints showed clearly. The man had done little to hide his tracks here, and Eagle Feather moved swiftly.

After a descent of about a thousand feet he came to a water storage tank. From it he had a fine view of the buildings and oil storage tanks beneath it. To Eagle Feather's eye, it was a complex network of strangely shaped buildings ranging from a small community of houses to some large storage tanks and a series of large diameter pipes sometimes running in parallel, sometimes intertwining like snakes. The man's tracks continued down toward the complex. Eagle Feather followed.

A large fence loomed with a twelve-foot gate chained with a large padlock and a sign prohibiting entry. The surface here was gravel and the tracks disappeared. Eagle Feather guessed the man had bypassed the gate, following the fence to the east side, then gone down into an arroyo where he could not be seen by anyone associated with the processing plant. Eagle Feather had started to follow when he heard a shout.

He saw a man in coveralls approaching along the fence.

"Hey, you, what are you doing here?"

Eagle Feather waited for him.

The man was burly with a broad face and a mat of dark curly hair. When he came close he repeated his question.

"What are you doing here? This is private property."

When Eagle Feather did not reply immediately the man said, "You'd best have a good reason or I'll turn you in." He removed a small walkie-talkie from a deep pocket in his coveralls.

Eagle Feather took a folded sheet of paper from his shirt pocket and handed it to him. "I work with the FBI. I am on the trail of a shooting suspect."

The man inspected the document and handed it back. "I haven't heard of any shooting."

"It happened in the State Park two days ago. The rifleman came back up over the ridge and down here." He pointed at the arroyo. "He went down there. Did you see anyone come down this way in the last two days?"

The man shook his head. "No. But I'm not always on duty here." He regarded Eagle Feather. "You just walked over the ridge from the park?"

Eagle Feather nodded. He looked around. "What is this place?"

"I guess you mean what was this place. It used to be a processing plant for the crude pumped from the offshore platforms. Chevron owned it. But it's been decommissioned."

"Was this plant involved with the pipeline?"

"Yeah, it was. We stored the crude, siphoned off the raw gas, warmed the oil and added butane and natural gas liquids and sent it on through the pipeline. But when the pipeline ruptured and spilled all that changed." He eyed Eagle Feather closely. "Say, you must not be from around here if you don't know all that."

"I was called in as part of a special team," Eagle Feather said. He studied the man. "Are you security?"

"Well, sort of. I'm overseeing what's left of the decommissioning process." He waved an arm toward the empty concrete pads beyond the fence. "Not much left here to watch, just empty tanks airing in the sun. The treatment, discharge and desalination units are idled."

"What was the desalination for?"

"It was used to create pure water for steam to raise the temperature of the crude. There is no mineral residue in it to contaminate the oil." He grinned. "I washed my truck with the stuff, it didn't leave any watermarks."

Eagle Feather changed the subject. "Do you know a man named Halligon?"

"John Halligon? From the pipeline company? Sure. Why?"

"The suspect I am tracking shot at him. He missed. Do you know why anyone would do that?"

"Shoot John? No, that's crazy. He's just a representative of the pipeline company. I think he's doing PR for them while they prepare to build their new line. I mean, sure, there's some people heated up about the spill and the whole issue of producing and transporting oil, but he's just doing a job." He squinted at Eagle Feather. "Hey, I heard about that woman's body they found up there. All burnt up, they say. Anything to do with that?"

Eagle Feather shrugged. "I cannot see how." He glanced down at the arroyo. "Where does that lead?"

The man followed his eyes. "The gully? That leads down to the sea, passes under the freeway. There are storage tanks down there, but they belong to a different company."

"This dismantling project is not new."

The man shook his head. "No, this has been going on for years. Now it's all about moving the oil inland to refineries. But like I said, the pipeline spill brought the oil and all the issues back into focus."

"This guy with the rifle? Any ideas?" Eagle Feather asked.

The man shrugged. "I got no idea." He grinned. "Any other questions?"

Eagle Feather knew it would take fifteen minutes to find where the man had parked his truck and driven away. He did not expect to learn anything new from continuing on. He shook his head, turned and started back up the slope.

"Hey, I'm knocking off just about now. I can give you a lift over to your vehicle."

Eagle Feather waved an arm. "No, thanks."

Once he regained the ridge, Eagle Feather glanced at the sun. He took out his phone to call Zack but reached his message service. "Ho, White Man. I will not make the meeting. I will come to find you at the hotel."

He put the phone away absently and stared out at the magnificent vista spread before him. The lowering orb of the sun shimmered on the Pacific and sent a bright widening path toward him, a giant search beam that lit the hillside beneath him and cast his shadow far into the saddle beyond. He gave a grunt and turned and retraced his earlier steps. Below the saddle the trail followed a narrow creek bed, more of a trough filled with rocks and deposits from runoff. It was slow going. At the fence separating National Forest from State Park, the trail widened and his pace increased. He took the Tunnel View trail and entered the Gaviota gap valley from the east. He arrived in fading light above the area where the mist warriors had arisen. He hesitated, then turned down the path to a point where he could study the boulders that had birthed them. At first glance they seemed randomly placed, scattered upon the grassy slope as if rolled down the hill in an outsized game of marbles. After a time, though, he thought he discerned a certain symmetry to them, a purposefulness like a graveyard of giant tombs. He knew spirits resided here, but why?

Eagle Feather's eyes shifted up to the skyline of the opposite ridge. The sun was sinking, the time of the spirits was fast approaching. He turned away, reluctant to disturb them further. When he could, he would talk to the Chumash elders about this place.

CHAPTER FIFTEEN

"We know who you are. We know why you came here. These are the keys you need to find your answers. Proceed at your own risk."

Zack stared at the two small keys on the desk where they had tumbled out when he opened the envelope. They looked like lockbox keys. One had a blue dot, the other red. He'd found the envelope on the desk in his room. It was addressed to him by name. He turned the typed message over, holding just an edge. Nothing else was written, no clue where the keys were meant to be used, no other information. He continued to stare at the letter as he placed it carefully on the desk and picked up the phone.

"McLeish, I think you need to see a letter I just received. Better bring a fingerprint kit."

He put down the phone and sat down to wait and to think about things. He'd spent the afternoon with Spud and McLeish interviewing the only two Vandenberg project chairmen who utilized paraffin and carbon black in their work and kept a supply on hand. Both had been curious, helpful, willing, yet secretive by the same measure. Zack figured secrecy was ingrained into their nature by now. They both claimed all fuel types and quantities used were carefully monitored and entered in a written log. Nothing seemed out of order to either man. They had strict budgets and were accountable for every expenditure. Neither was utilizing any fuel in an open flame situation. Both men were sent away having pledged to double their vigilance.

Zack had raised Eagle Feather's point with Spud that the fuel mixture could be found at the airfield for use by jets. He questioned the appropriate officers and learned that all fuel mixtures used there are specified by the Air Force and come premixed from military sources. The base uses JP-8 fuel for all jets unless otherwise specified, and all mixes include corrosion inhibitors and anti-icing chemicals. All of this information left Zack with his head spinning and a feeling the investigation at Vandenberg was going nowhere.

But this envelope with the note and the keys changed everything. Somewhere along the line they had stirred a pot enough to induce the note writer to reach out to him. His room had been invaded twice now. Was it by the same person? He was convinced the first intruder had been after the rifle shell. Could the rifleman's bullet actually have been meant for Zack, not Halligon? If so, how had that person known Zack would be there at that particular time? According to Eagle Feather, the shooter had made a long and arduous trek to the site of the shooting. How could anyone possibly have planned such a trek around such a narrow and quite random window?

Zack shook his head. None of it made sense. He glanced at his watch, decided to check with the desk clerk to see if he knew anything about the note. He didn't expect much, though.

He was right. The clerk knew nothing, had not authorized a key to anyone, had not seen anyone unusual near the elevator and he certainly had not brought the note himself. As Zack turned away, McLeish entered the lobby. They took the elevator up to the room.

Before entering, McLeish examined the electronic lock and dusted the area around it, then recorded his findings. He decided to dust the entire room. As he worked his way from one likely location to another they discussed the case.

McLeish had a lot of questions. "Are we talking about more than one person here? Is this a cause of some sort with a group involved? Or is the reference in the note the royal "we"? Male? Female?"

Zack shook his head. "My gut tells me we have one male with a big ego. More, if the shooter and the killer are one and the same, his knowledge of the back trails in the region suggests a local. According to Eagle Feather, his path to the site was a long and difficult one."

McLeish nodded. "Local and quite fit." He raised an eyebrow. "Didn't you say the lady at the historical society described a man she had helped to research the Las Cruces history as looking fit? Something about a military bearing?"

"That's right, she did." Zack ticked the points off on his fingers. "We've got a military man, someone familiar with weapons, very fit, and from her description at least forty but not older than fifty or fifty-five."

"That doesn't narrow our choices much around a military base," McLeish said.

"Maybe it does if we think of him as local. Either that or he's been deployed here a long time."

"Long enough to become familiar with the trails," McLeish said.

Zack nodded. "He's also apparently got access to accurate and timely information about our comings and goings. Who could even know I was coming? The FBI? Spud's department? Base flight information? Anyone else?"

McLeish grimaced. "The pool does widen as you talk about it. Anyone at your end?"

Zack shook his head. "Just my boss. Libby knew, but she didn't know any details."

McLeish had finished the room and was now working with the letter. He worked quietly, then glanced at Zack. "Well, I've taken finger prints around the room. We'll run them all. But there is nothing on this envelope, the letter, or the keys except for a portion of a print on the edge of the letter and two on the envelope all of which I suspect belong to you, Zack."

"Why am I not surprised?"

McLeish gave a wry grin. "Now for our next challenge."

"Right. We need to figure out what those keys open." Zack picked them up, bounced them in his palm. "They could be keys to a gym locker, like at a club. Let's see if the manager has any ideas."

When they approached the day clerk, he looked at the keys and immediately shook his head. "No, those wouldn't fit anything here. We use electronic cards almost exclusively." He picked up the desk phone. "Just a minute." He dialed a three digit number.

Moments later, the manager appeared at the door behind the desk and invited them into her office. When she heard Zack's story, she became upset. "Someone has broken into your room? We need to call the police!"

McLeish shook his head. "No, that won't be necessary." He showed her his credentials. "We are involved in a case and this incident is probably linked to it. We can't afford publicity. However, I very much doubt this person will return." He handed her the keys. "We would like to learn something about these keys. Locker or mailbox keys often have a free mailer with an address to return it, but there is nothing like that on these. And the color coding seems unusual. Do they suggest anything to you?"

She studied them, handed them back. "No, I can assure you they don't fit anything in this hotel. I have not seen these keys before."

"Thank you for your time," Zack said. "Please ask your staff not to mention this incident. We can guarantee the safety of your guests if no one discusses the break-in. As my colleague said, this person will not repeat the action."

As they crossed the lobby, McLeish asked, "Where next?"

"The Air Force Base. I want Spud to take a look at these. They arrived after our day of interviews over there."

Spud responded to Zack's call saying he would be in his office. They went to the base.

When the two FBI agents arrived he waved them in.

"Back so soon? I thought you'd be discouraged after yesterday."

Zack gave an unhappy shake of his head. "I am. But I wanted you to look at these." He handed the keys to Spud.

Spud looked at them, glanced up at Zack. "Locker keys? Mailbox? Padlocks? What's with these?"

Zack grunted. "I hoped they might be familiar to you. They were in an envelope left in my room along with a note. It said the keys were our answer."

Spud studied them closely. "They both have PF inscribed near the top, you can just see it. Might be the maker. I have no idea about the blue and red dots." He threw up his hands. "Do you know how many lockers, lock boxes, gates, padlocks, cabinets, or whatever there are on this base? These could belong to anybody, anywhere, public or private. Not much help, I'm afraid." He handed them back to Zack. "Is there any particular reason they belong here more than anywhere else?"

Zack shook his head. "Not really. Worth a shot, though."

"This guy would not have sent those keys to you if he didn't think you'd figure out where to use them," McLeish said. "Keep them in your pocket. Somewhere along the way they'll fit in."

Spud's desk phone rang. He spoke quietly into it for a moment, hung it up. He gave Zack a big grin. "There is someone at the gate to see you. They're bringing her around now."

"Her?"

Spud shrugged. "That's all they said. But she impressed the gate guard enough to send her in."

Zack was still puzzling out who this might be when a knock sounded on the door and a tall broad shouldered guard filled it.

"You visitor, sir."

The guard stood aside and a woman moved gracefully yet assertively into the room. She stood and glanced at each of them in turn, her body erect, her hair lustrously full and dark, smiling with perfect white teeth in sparkling contrast to the dark pools that were her eyes. Her hair was done up in a bun, she wore a business-like pant suit and white collared shirt which might as well have been a ballroom gown in terms of her impact on the men in the room.

Zack heard a collective intake of breath. He made a clumsy gesture with an arm. "My boss, gentlemen. Agent Janice Hooper."

Janice nodded to Zack and extended a hand to McLeish. "How are you today, James?" She approached Spud, now standing behind his desk. "You must be Agent Spud Jarvis. I've heard so much about you." White teeth flashed and dark eyes shimmered as she spoke.

Spud came around the desk to take her hand. She took it, smiling, and turned to face them all and in so doing usurping Spud's position at the desk.

"We have much to talk about, gentlemen," she said. "Please sit down."

She went and sat in Spud's chair assuming the power position behind the desk as if it were the most natural thing in the world. Spud scrambled to find another seat.

Janice put on her brightest smile. "From all I can see, you've all made a right fig of this investigation so far. Am I right?"

"Well—" McLeish began.

"Have you any real leads?"

Zack spoke quickly. He knew where this could go. "We know who created the fiery dancer spectacle for the motorists."

Brown eyes glistened at him. "That was solved by the Indian Who Does Not Exist, am I right? He is not even an official part of this team." She didn't pause. "You, James, had a body burned to cinder and left for all to see. Almost a taunt, I would say. What are the who, what, where, how, and why?"

"Oh, well, the 'who', well, we don't actually know that yet. The 'what' is a burned body, the 'where' is on a grassy knoll above the Ortega Trail in Gaviota State Park, the 'how' is with paraffin and carbon black, and the 'why'...uh, well, we don't actually know that yet."

"Isn't that pretty much what we knew when we started the case?" Janice was still smiling, her voice honey coated but Zack had seen that smile before and wasn't fooled. "Zack, I had you sent out here to help resolve this case. Instead, you seem to be running in circles. Why did someone shoot at the oilman, John Halligon?"

"There might have been a number of reasons, for instance—"

"Are we sure the shooter intended to shoot Halligon, and not, say, you?"

"Well, I—"

"Given the fact an anonymous person directed a letter to you regarding the case along with a warning, don't you think you might be high on the target list?"

"Well, I suppose—"

The desk chair squeaked as she turned it to face Spud. "Despite all your help, Agent Jarvis, for which we are grateful, it seems likely the fuel used to burn our victim did not come from Vandenberg Air Force Base. The latest analysis from our lab, the results of which should be in your phone, Agent McLeish, show a less refined kerosene than one might expect through conventional refinement processes." Janice gave a special smile for McLeish. "In other words, we are looking for homemade kerosene, not something available from distributors."

"Home distilled," Spud said.

"Exactly."

"You'd need a retort furnace, or at least a deep pit with a big distilling tower."

She nodded. "Are you a chemist, Agent Jarvis?"

"Specializing in oil, coal, and shale byproducts as they apply to jet and rocket fuels, yes."

"Then you will be a huge help to these gentlemen, I would imagine." She stood, centered herself in the room, looked at the faces of each man in turn. "This investigation needs to move swiftly. There are too many cultural and political bombs ready to explode. Fingers are already pointing at the Chumash, the oil industry, the oil protestors, and a whole slate of environmentalist groups. Let's narrow the choices quickly, please."

Janice nodded to the guard and swept from the room.

CHAPTER SIXTEEN

Zack's phone rang just as he was pulling off his boots. It was Eagle Feather.

"I am sorry I missed your meeting."

"It didn't happen quite the way I expected. Agent Hooper, my boss, showed up. You would have enjoyed the way Janice ripped a stripe off of us."

Eagle Feather chuckled. "Yes, I would have liked that."

"Trouble is, she was right. We have nothing. The lab now believes the accelerant used to burn the woman was homemade. The air base may not be involved after all." He gave a long sigh.

"You need fresh ideas, White Man. I am at the reservation. You should come see me."

"Now?"

"It is only six. I think you need to be revitalized."

Zack agreed. Following Eagle Feather's directions, he turned off the highway into the main casino entrance, drove around to the back of the building and into the parking garage. Then he took the elevator to the retail shop level and walked from there through the crowded casino to the coffee shop. He spotted Eagle Feather waving from a corner table.

"I didn't expect to find you in these surroundings," Zack said, gazing at the constant motion in the casino beyond the glass. The dings, dongs, and musical snippets of the machines were a constant background noise.

Eagle Feather grinned. "This is where I eat unless I visit the Buffet. We should do that together one time. It is excellent."

"Where does your friend live?"

Eagle Feather pointed skyward. "He lives near the top of the tower. He manages this place."

A waitress approached with two beers and a bowl of pretzels.

"I ordered for both of us."

Zack hoisted his beer against Eagle Feather's. "You did well, my friend." His eyes flicked from one glittery spectacle to the next across the vast gaming room. "I must say, you constantly surprise me."

"Let me try to surprise you again. The man I followed today is about six feet tall, longer in the legs than the torso, wears a size ten shoe, and has dark brown hair. He has large hands, is very strong. I would guess his hands are calloused, which would suggest hard work with tools. I—"

"Wait a minute, Eagle Feather. Did you see him? Did you find him?"

Eagle Feather looked amused. "I did not see him except in my mind's eye. I trailed him, remember."

Zack shook his head slowly. "I know your powers, my friend, but calloused hands? Dark hair?"

"The man snapped a large scaly branch and grabbed rough rock surfaces but left no sign of scrapes. He left finger imprints in the dirt, he did not wear gloves. His hands are tough. I found a hair where he removed his hat and rubbed his head."

"Oh, I see."

Eagle Feather stared at him. "Yes, you do now."

Zack held up both palms apologetically. "Do go on."

"He wore a hiking boot. He does not wear glasses, his eyesight is excellent. He is a woodsman accustomed to traveling long distances on foot over rough ground."

Zack leaned back in his chair. "Where did he go?"

"He went over the summit ridge and down the slope toward the oil storage plant and the freeway. He may have left a vehicle there."

"May have? You didn't check?"

Eagle Feather shook his head. "I told you he is a woodsman. He would not have left signs to show me that much. So I turned back. Why waste my time?"

He paused, looked at Zack. "Why do you think he shot at the oil man?"

"We don't know who he intended to shoot," Zack said. "Or why."

Eagle Feather was silent.

Zack sipped his beer.

After a few moments, Eagle Feather said, "I think he shot at the oil man."

"Halligon."

"Yes. Halligon had a job, he had a routine. The shooter had to be sure he was there. No one would hike such a distance over such terrain unless he was sure his target would be there."

"That is what I thought, until the keys."

"Keys? What keys?"

Zack told Eagle Feather about the envelope with the note and keys.

"That proves it then," Eagle Feather said. "If he left the note after the shooting, he had only just learned you were here. His shot was intended to scare the oil man, not someone he didn't know would be there."

"Scare, not hit?"

Eagle Feather nodded, his face solemn. "Scare. Such a woodsman would not miss an easy shot like that."

Zack rubbed his palm across his forehead, thinking about it. At the next table, a woman with a high-pitched voice was reliving her experience with a one-armed bandit for her companion. The smell of hamburger filled the room.

"Supposing you are right, he must have had a powerful motive. It's a long way to hike just to miss."

"To send a message."

"About?"

"Something to do with oil, or maybe the pipeline? Wasn't this man in charge of pipeline security?" Eagle Feather sipped his beer.

Zack stared at him. "My boss spoke of all the factions with an interest in the new pipeline. Environmentalists, water resources protectors, rare species protectors, landowners, and archaeological site protectors." He sipped his beer, looked at Eagle Feather. "Was it the Chumash? An outdoorsman, with that kind of skill?"

Eagle Feather shook his head. "I do not think so. The tribe has learned that is not the way to get things done."

"Yet the kids, those laser lights..."

"Those were kids. This is not a kid. This is a man, a very purposeful man."

Zack reached into his pocket, pulled out the keys and dumped them on the table. "What do you make of these?" When Eagle Feather hesitated, he said, "You can handle them, the forensics man has all he needs."

Eagle Feather picked them up and studied them. "They are almost the same."

"Same manufacturer, no doubt. But you see the keyed edges are just slightly different. They open two different locks."

"A pair of lockers? A storage facility?"

Zack shrugged. "Who knows?"

"But this person wants you to find where these go, otherwise why send them?"

"Exactly."

"It must seem obvious to him."

Zack frowned. "How could it?"

Eagle Feather put down his beer. "If we assume it is one and the same person, we know he spends much time outdoors. We know he shot at a pipeline security man, therefore he wanted to cause alarm. Why? To slow the progress of the new pipeline? We know the body was burned with some sort of homemade kerosene. Where? How was that made?"

"I am told it can be made with crude oil or shale. It requires a furnace of high heat capacity and a certain amount of distillation, like a tower. It can be made in brick retort ovens, like the old days."

"Could this be done underground?"

"I should think it could be done underground using earth as a muffler and insulator."

Eagle Feather nodded. "Maybe instead of looking high in the air for rockets we should look underground for earthen ovens."

The thought brought a momentary silence to the conversation.

Zack's phone rang. It was McLeish.

"'Zack, where are you?"

"I'm at the casino with Eagle Feather."

"Well, you'd better drop your chips and come out here. I'm on my way to Las Cruces. There's been a large explosion. The early news is it was a high pressure gas line that blew up."

CHAPTER SEVENTEEN

Zack saw the glow of the fire before they were even close. Darkness had settled in but beyond the lights of Buellton a reddish glow outlined the high mountain ridges and a voluminous cloud cast the sky a murky shade. There was no traffic approaching in the northbound lanes. As they began the long ride up the final ridge before the descent into the gorge the traffic in their lanes slowed and finally stopped altogether.

Zack turned into the far right truck lane and when that became filled with impatient drivers he put on his flashers and rolled along the shoulder, but even that maneuver failed.

The whop-whop roar of a helicopter sounded above them.

His phone rang. It was McLeish. "Zack, I see you. I've got a black and white coming to lead you in."

Before long they saw blue and red flashes reflecting off vehicles in front of them and a patrol car neared, edging vehicles away from the shoulder. It stopped up ahead at a wide place and reversed direction and an officer stepped out as they pulled up. "Good evening, sir," he said. "I've been assigned to lead you to the temporary command center."

They followed the patrol car down the long grade into the gap area. The fire was clearer now, the roar of helicopters and low flying aircraft almost deafening. The highway patrol were turning traffic across the median to reverse their direction, away from the conflagration.

As they neared the intersection of U.S. 101 with California Route 1, areas of intense flame became distinct. Several hulks that had been automobiles were mounds of flame on the roadway. A tower of fire gushed up from the gas line. On the eastern slope a line of fire ate its way upward. Fire trucks lined the freeway overpass in front of them and hoses tangled on the macadam as far as they could see.

The patrol car led them down the exit ramp and off it onto a widened dirt parking area at a road maintenance storage facility. But tonight it was filled with official vehicles, flashing lights, and men looking at maps spread on vehicle hoods while others held phones and radios.

The patrol car in front of them stopped and Zack parked the Jeep behind it. Just as he stepped out a jet plane released a chemical drop with a tremendous whoosh and a deafening roar against the eastern slope. Zack automatically cringed against the side of his vehicle. He could feel tiny droplets as from a wet fog.

"Jesus Christ!" The officer walking back toward them had almost been knocked off his feet by the gust it caused. He motioned them to follow him.

McLeish found them, whispered something in the officer's ear and gestured Zack and Eagle Feather to follow him to his car. They piled in. It was relatively quiet and they could talk without shouting.

"What caused this?" Zack asked. But in his heart he knew the answer.

McLeish's face was grim. "They don't know yet. No one can get near the source, won't be able to until the gas is off and the fire around it under control. But according to the fire chief, the initial blast was almost horizontal, shooting flame across the freeway onto the eastern slope. That was followed by an enormous explosion that dug a crater into the hillside and halfway across the freeway. That's what happened to those poor bastards." He pointed toward the burning vehicles. "As the pipe ripped open the blast went vertical as well." He looked at Zack. "So, yes, one likely cause is a bullet from a high-powered rifle fired from the east slope."

"Would a bullet actually ignite the gas?" Eagle Feather asked.

"I wondered that too," McLeish said. "Wouldn't the blast of gas be too powerful for any spark to ignite it?"

Zack grunted. "If he used traditional ammo, maybe. But there is special ammo that would do the trick."

"Would he need a special weapon for that?" Eagle Feather asked.

McLeish shook his head. "Not necessarily. He can get incendiary ammo for his .308. It's illegal in California, but not in forty-eight other states." He shrugged.

"If so, the shooter may have torched himself from that initial blast," Zack said, staring out the window. He was awestruck by the enormity of the catastrophe.

Eagle Feather was watching the line of fire marching up the hill. "No," he said. "If he planned this, I think he was above the place the flames started. I think he escaped."

"I guess we won't know the answer to that one for a while, either." McLeish said. "One good thing, an automatic valve closure prevented any further explosions upstream."

Even as he spoke, the fiery gusher diminished and began receding like a sprinkler hose turning off. The sudden retreat of the bright light left them semi blinded.

"Guess they just got the main valve turned off."

As their eyes adjusted, they could see the fire on the west slope for the first time. There was no organized march of flame as on the opposite wall, just scattered areas of burning.

"It is a good thing there is not much wind tonight," Eagle Feather said.

"It'll be a busy night for the firemen regardless." Zack's words were accompanied by another whoosh of a retardant drop. He turned to Eagle Feather. "Supposing someone did shoot this pipeline and supposing it is the same guy you tracked, could we catch him now if he is trying to escape?"

Eagle Feather shook his head. "The last time he entered from the oil facility, which is on the other side of the fire from us. There is no way we can get there by car now. Even if we could, he might have come in another way. There are too many possibilities."

McLeish grunted. "Anybody here doubt this was our man? He already took a shot at Halligon." He grunted again. "He might even have been aiming for the pipe right then."

Zack rubbed his cheek, feeling the beard getting scratchy just from the long day. Morning seemed a long time ago. "I think he hit exactly what he aimed at that time. He shot a chunk out of the tree as a warning to Halligon. Tonight he hit the pipe. That says to me he warned Halligon about something, Halligon didn't listen, and now this."

McLeish turned to stare at Zack. "You think Halligon actually knows the shooter?"

"I think we need to talk to him, at least."

McLeish was staring at the flames. "I wonder where Halligon is with all this going on?"

"If I was his boss, he'd be on the carpet in front of me right now," Zack said.

"Let's find out." McLeish picked up his phone, called the CHP incident commander, talked for a few minutes, hung up. "He'll call me back if he can find Halligon."

"Nothing more we can do sitting here," Zack said. "Let's go back to the Marriott and plan our next steps."

* * * * *

Zack's room became the war room. He stretched out on his bed on his back, legs crossed. McLeish sat in the bedroom chair while Eagle Feather straddled the desk chair turned backward, his arms crossed across the seat back.

McLeish looked at his phone. "I just got a message from the CHP. I've got Halligon's cell number now. Shall we call him?"

"Yeah, make an appointment for tomorrow. We need to have eyes on his reactions when we speak to him."

McLeish got Halligon's message service, asked for a call back, explained they'd like an interview. After he was done, they stared at each other.

"Without the Halligon connection, what have we got?" Zack asked.

McLeish shrugged. "Well, not much. They've managed to extract some DNA from the burned corpse. But we need someone to compare it to."

Zack glanced at Eagle Feather, then back at McLeish. "You had the lab look for finger prints on the brass we found on the hillside, remember? What about DNA?"

McLeish shook his head. "No. At the time, that wasn't our thinking. They looked for fingerprints, didn't find any. But I didn't ask about DNA. I'll put them on that tomorrow."

Zack crossed his legs the other way, thinking. "If we suppose we've got some guy out there trying to stop the progress of the pipeline, he must be pretty desperate to risk his life and the lives of others to do it. Why?"

McLeish gave a grim smile. "There's people out there putting themselves in harms way all the time for the environment. How about those crazy guys on the rubber rafts getting in the way of those huge Japanese whaling boats?"

"This feels more determined to me, more personal."

"Maybe the pipeline threatens something that belongs to him," Eagle Feather said.

McLeish shook his head. "I don't see how. For one thing, this pipeline will follow the path of the original quite closely except to move out of urban neighborhoods like western Buellton. For another, the land it will cross is either state owned or private ranch land. Those are all big ranches, and I'm sure sufficient palms were slapped to keep everybody happy there. I just don't see what it could be other than political."

"What about the murder? If that has anything to do with the pipeline other than a coincidence of its location, it is a very large statement," Zack said. "The symbolic burning of the woman with the hoops points a finger directly toward an event in history. We can't forget that."

"Zack is right," Eagle Feather said. "We are missing something here that has to do with the 1864 Corliss murder."

Zack leaned forward. "Look, even though the exact cause of the murder is still debated, there is no doubt the land belonged to the Corliss descendants, at least until the 1888 judgment. If I understand it correctly, that judgment hinged on the details of the Corliss murder, specifically which person died last. When it was judged to be unknowable and therefore simultaneous, the Corliss parcel, a ninth of the original grant, I believe, disappeared into the Hollister estate and later was sold to the state." Zack glanced at McLeish. "So the DNA comparison, if they can do it, might be significant. There could be a compelling motive there."

McLeish looked doubtful. "That's a long time to harbor a grudge."

"But new events, such as restructuring a pipeline through land that someone feels should rightfully belong to him might stir the embers."

McLeish shrugged, unconvinced.

Eagle Feather stood. "White men enjoy debating hypothetical situations. I prefer facts—and sleep."

Zack looked up at his friend from under his brows. "You seem to be getting plenty of sleep lately. You must be enjoying your suite at the casino."

"It is quite comfortable." Eagle Feather turned toward the door.

"Is that all?"

The Navajo turned to look back at Zack. "What exactly do you mean, White Man?"

"Just asking."

Eagle Feather stared for a moment, then closed the door firmly behind him.

CHAPTER EIGHTEEN

The next day the news was all about the tragic explosion and fire in the gap. By seven that morning as Zack, Eagle Feather, and McLeish sat down at Ellen's for breakfast the body count was seven with four more severely injured. Five cars, several vans and a semi had been immolated by the blast. A film segment that showed a driver beating out flames with his jacket on a tandem oil rig that had just narrowly escaped the explosion was played again and again.

The fire's advance had been stopped on the east slope not far beyond where it had been when the men left last night thanks to minimal wind and quick action on the part of the firemen and the coordinated air drops. They would be busy today putting out spot fires on both slopes, but the crises was over for now.

Zack twisted his head to see the single small TV screen set up on the end of the counter by the restaurant manager. A reporter was interviewing a representative of the gas pipeline.

"We can't say for sure how this occurred," the oil man was saying, shaking his head. *"Our instruments registered a sudden and immediate drop in pressure at the location of the explosion. There was no indication of a valve leak or any other sort of malfunction that might cause such a release of gas. This was an instantaneous rending of the insulation and casing."*

"Could it have come from a weakness in the pipe, perhaps material eroded over the years?"

"No chance."

"What could cause it, then?"

The oil representative put up palms. *"Only a sudden, strong impact from the exterior of the pipe."*

The reporter looked at the camera, then at the oil man. *"Could a bullet have done it?"*

The oil rep hesitated. *"That possibility can not be dismissed."*

Zack turned away from the screen and looked at his breakfast companions. "The less the public knows about that, the better."

McLeish nodded in agreement. "I've sent a message to the lab. They'll prioritize processing the DNA from the shell casing if they can find enough. It will still take several hours for even an initial finding." He looked at Zack. "What now? We're about out of paths to follow."

"Did we learn anything from the burnt woman's DNA?"

McLeish shook his head. "Nothing. It doesn't match anything in our files, doesn't match the Corliss family at all. Until we find a match, it's useless."

"Why not follow the pipeline," Eagle Feather said in the silence that followed.

McLeish looked at him. "What do you mean?"

Zack raised an eyebrow. "You mean physically?"

Eagle Feather nodded.

McLeish frowned. "You mean tramp through the brush and stuff? Good god, why?"

Zack gave a slow nod. "To see what it is this man wants to protect."

"For god's sake, look at a map. Or better yet, Google Earth."

Zack shook his head. "That won't tell us everything we need to know." He dug in his pocket, held up his palm. The two locker keys lay there. "This guy has something locked away. He gave us the clue himself. I think Eagle Feather is right. I think we'll find it somewhere along the pipeline route—the new pipeline route."

McLeish was beginning to understand. "You may be on to something. I'll get a map of the proposed pipeline."

Zack was already rising from the table, a hand on Eagle Feather's shoulder. "Put on some hiking boots, grab a water bottle and a sandwich." He looked at McLeish. "We'll meet at my room at the Marriott in a half hour."

Eagle Feather followed Zack's Cherokee to the Marriott. Everything he needed for any outdoor activity was already in his rusty red truck, where he kept it.

The two friends relaxed in Zack's room as they waited for McLeish. They hadn't had much time together since the case began.

"How is Libby?" Eagle Feather had known Zack before his marriage, back in the time Libby ran her own ranch and trained bloodhounds. He had known Libby even before he met Zack.

"She is well...and happier, I think. My current arrangement with the FBI is working out for us. This case is my first extended stay away from the family since I accepted Agent Hooper's offer to return to the agency." He grinned. "That's behind her surprise visit here, I'm sure. She wants to be sure it's all going well."

"It is her butt on the line."

Zack laughed. "Exactly." His eyes narrowed as he regarded his friend. "Speaking of women, what's going on back at the casino with you? You scoot back over there every evening as soon as you can get away. Has someone caught your eye there?"

"White Man, I think you have spent too much time looking for mysteries. You see them where they do not exist."

Zack had opened his mouth to respond when a knock sounded. He looked at Eagle Feather as he walked to the door. "Saved by the bell this time, my friend."

It was McLeish. He had his laptop under his arm and walked directly to the desk and opened it. "I have here the complete map of the proposed new pipeline as registered with the counties of Santa Barbara, San Luis Obispo, and Kern." He struck a few keys, then swung the laptop so everyone could see the screen. Zack and Eagle Feather clustered around.

"This red line is the proposed route. As you can see, it stays largely within the state park after leaving the coast until it reaches Route 1. There it follows the U.S. 101 freeway north except for this wide swing west around Buellton." McLeish traced it with the cursor. "Whatever this guy is concerned about could be anywhere along there. You fellows will be in the bush a long time."

"You will not be joining us?" Eagle Feather asked.

Zack thought he saw a twinkle in his friend's eye.

McLeish flashed a quick grin in return. "I think you boys are more than capable on your own. I'll act as home base for you. That said, how do you intend to narrow your search to a reasonable area?"

"I think we have some clues," Zack said. "All of his activities have been in the gap area. He clearly knows the trails in and around the state park extremely well."

Eagle Feather reached a hand toward the map and extended a finger. "Here is where he was when he shot at Halligon. He probably shot the gas line from the same place. But the new pipeline is way up there." His finger swept west up the slope to the ridgeline. "Maybe the gas pipe was his concern."

Zack considered this. "It's true, there has been no talk of the gas line, just the high pressure oil pipeline because of the spill. But the gas line has been there a long time and there aren't, or maybe I should say there weren't any plans to move it. The burned body imitating the historic murder, the Chumash youngsters and their laser projection and the shootings all began following the pipeline oil spill and subsequent plans to build another. That's why I think this guy's problem is with the new oil pipeline." He looked at McLeish. "Can we find a similar map showing the old pipeline route? We could then focus on the points of deviation."

"You mean look for new areas they intend to dig up."

"Exactly."

"I have heard they will affect a wide area of land on either side of the pipe," Eagle Feather said. "I think this project will be disruptive everywhere along its path, old or new."

McLeish nodded. "I think you're right."

Zack threw his hands in the air. "If we don't use points of deviation, where do we start?"

"What are we looking for?" Eagle Feather asked.

"Something that requires two keys to unlock it."

"Like a safety deposit box," McLeish grumbled.

"Yes, I take your point," Zack said, a little exasperated. "This does feel like a hunch that might lead us on a wild goose chase. But where else do we start?"

"It could be a gate," Eagle Feather said. "There are many ranch gates around here, some have more than one lock."

"Or an outer and inner gate."

"So what is he protecting?" McLeish asked. "It wouldn't be just pasture. What's worth committing a symbolic murder to protect?"

"A mine, maybe? Gold, or silver? That would be worth it."

Eagle Feather nodded. "A large marijuana operation, maybe."

Zack shifted the computer screen to look closely at it and enlarged the picture. "Let's not forget the original Corliss murder piece of the puzzle. The Corliss's owned a ninth portion of Las Cruces. That disappeared. For descendants, the loss of land can be a motivator, although murder and blowing up pipelines seems extreme. We know the original land was for sheep grazing, not for mining or growing marijuana. Of course, someone could have come along and begun either. We know with relative certainty where the original Corliss land was." Zack traced a finger across the pipeline map exposing the underlay of relief. "It was north of the narrowest gap section. The accounts show they built a new building on the stage road just north of the gap indicating their first home was somewhere else. But the road divided near the old Las Cruces Adobe, just as it does now, which was why the Williams brothers who were living there and had also bid on the franchise were so confident. Their location was compelling."

"Where are you going with this history lesson, White Man?"

Zack turned to his own laptop, opened it, and began opening documents. He pointed to the screen. "Look. This is the diseño accepted by the Americans in 1883. The Corliss's came in 1860 and died in 1864. Look at this map. There is no sign of their ever having lived here." He waved a hand across the image. "A ninth is a very large chunk. Corliss could have owned everything south of the road divide, for instance. But we see old Vicente Corderos' house here and his vineyards in the divide area and the hot springs, which is up this draw behind his house. We know Corliss never owned that property. But take that property away, and the remaining portion south of the road division is too small to be a ninth. So I think Corliss owned this area north and west of there along the boundary as well." He pointed to the other computer. "Now look at that pipeline map. If I am correct, the new pipeline will pass through the old Corliss property along these high ridges from here"—he stabbed a finger on the screen—"to here. That's where we need to search." He folded his arms and waited for a response. He got one.

"What are we waiting for, White Man. The sun is already high."

CHAPTER NINETEEN

Over the next few days Irma Jean felt her outrage diminish and with it her resistance to the idea they bury her mother close by. In a holistic way it made sense. After all, it would be good to know she was there, part of the soil they had tilled and planted, still part of their little farm as she had been before she passed. Bill assured Irma Jean the pipeline might be months, years, maybe not at all.

When she married Bill, she had seen him not just as a husband but as a partner. She admired and shared his independent ideas, his way of thinking outside the box, his resistance to the constraints from the culture that surrounded them. She realized her fond vision of a church funeral with weeping guests consoling her, the solace of music and words, her mother's coffin lowered into sacred soil could never be. As Bill had said, who would come? Where would the service be? Where would they bury her that held any meaning? They had chosen to leave all of that behind, had lived away from such societal connections for too long.

And so they had said the words they needed to say, standing together hand in hand looking down at her dead mother where she lay on the bed. They had remembered the good moments, the funny things, the silly things, the things that had drawn them all together. Then Bill had taken the body away. He would cremate her and her ashes would be spread all over the farm and her spirit would be with them always.

"Always," Bill had repeated, his jaw set.

Irma Jean had few friends. Bill never encouraged visitors to the farm. He changed their telephone number frequently, as he explained, to avoid fraud and nuisance calls, but also, she knew, to prevent the local company from billing them even though they used their own power. In the early days, she would drive out to see childhood and college friends. Now, they had all moved on with their lives and contact was rare. The farm animals, the dogs, the barn cats were her companions now that her mother was gone.

Bill had always been her true companion, but he was away a lot these days. He often returned home late at night, his clothing sweaty and dirty. He brushed off her questions with vague answers. When he wasn't away, he was in his workshop in the barn. Irma Jean knew not to disturb him there. He seldom smiled these days. Neither did she.

A week or so after her mother died, Bill told Irma Jean about the burnt body along the Ortega Trail in Goleta State Park. He had heard it on the news when checking the weather. Not much left, just some bones. Some sort of ritual, maybe. He saw the alarm in her eyes and tried to calm her. "Nothing to do with us. Nobody knows we're here or even cares." But Irma Jean was not reassured. Although violence was something beyond her experience, the thought of it frightened her. Neither she nor Bill ate meat. She wouldn't permit the thought of eating one of the farm animals, even when one died of old age. The local predators—bears, mountain lions, wildcats, coyotes— were kept at bay with trip wire whistles and noises. Bill had a rifle "just in case." Irma Jean knew in her heart the phrase he used had more to do with humans than animals. She suffered many bad nights thinking of those burnt bones and what they might mean.

Irma Jean knew the Ortega Trail. The trails of Goleta State Park were not so far away. She and Bill had walked them in the early days. She admired the ferocious beauty of the gap where the highway carved through, the cragged rock faces and deep dark ravines slashing into the mountainside. The terrain symbolized for her the true rawness of nature she loved.

The man Halligon showed up at the gate again a day or two later. He seemed agitated. Bill was busy in the barn. Irma Jean brought Halligon to the porch to wait while she summoned her husband. He came right over. The two men walked out into the meadow out of hearing. Irma Jean could tell they were angry by the tension in their bodies and the short sharp movements of their arms as they talked.

After the oil man left Bill was disgruntled. He told her Halligon had repeated his insistence they should prepare to leave.

"But you said—"

"What I told you is still true. It would be politically convenient for the pipeline company if the proposed path was clear. They want all of their ducks in a row well in advance. But I'm not going to make it so easy for them." He gave her the first tender look she'd seen from him in weeks. "Your mother will rest in peace. I promise you."

Irma Jean was relieved.

Two days later as Irma Jean prepared supper, there was a great boom and a rumbling underfoot. Her mind quickly categorized the possibilities—earthquake, rocket launch from nearby Vandenberg Air Base—but none quite fit. Bill was away, as usual. She had prepared supper for both of them in the hope he'd arrive back in time. The tremor underfoot took several seconds to stop. She finally concluded it had to be an earthquake. She'd experienced many and even though no two were ever exactly alike, this one felt very different. She ate her dinner in solitude, finally wrapped up Bill's dinner and put it away. He didn't return that night. He wasn't beside her when she woke the following morning. By late morning her imagination was filling her brain with numerous alarming scenarios. Despite his wanderings of late, he had never been gone this long before. She thought of the earthquake the night before, and her anxiety grew. She kept busy with mundane morning tasks but some instinctive warning bell sounded within her. At noon two men she had never seen before stood on her front walk.

CHAPTER TWENTY

The four drilling platforms that crouched with stingers deep into the ocean floor several miles out in the Pacific off Point Conception had been paused. After the leak, without the feeder pipeline, the complex conveyor belt that normally transported a steady stream of oil from those wells more than a hundred miles north and east through three counties to Pentland in Kern County was stopped. Truck transport from the Los Flores facility had increased proportionately, but now that the freeway was closed through the gap following the gas explosion the trucks would have to find another route.

The large diameter gas pipeline charged with two hundred pounds pressure had ruptured at a particularly critical place just prior to a smaller diameter branch pipe that conveyed gas to the communities to the east—Solvang, Santa Ynez, Ballard and Buellton. The flow of natural gas to all communities north and east of the explosion including Santa Maria and even Vandenberg Air Force Base had now ceased. Some areas may have to do without the fuel for a long time. The eight o'clock news had been filled with newspersons explaining the short and long term implications of the loss.

McLeish wondered about this as he researched the pipelines on his laptop while Zack and Eagle Feather prepared for their day in the bush. "Do you think this nut could have known the massive damage his one bullet would do?"

Zack didn't think so. "My guess? He was just lucky. But if he wanted attention, he's got it now."

As Zack threw items into a small backpack, Eagle Feather was busy superimposing the proposed pipeline schematic onto a relief map of the Las Cruces area. Once satisfied it was accurate, he sent it down to the printer in the business lounge on the first floor, then went to find the printout.

McLeish went his own way to follow up on a few details but announced he remain alert for a call from his colleagues should they need him.

Zack and Eagle Feather made their first stop at Burrito Loco for something to pack away for lunch. After that they drove to the freeway entrance. Zack slowed the vehicle to show his credentials to the patrolman who was waving cars away from the southbound ramp. All traffic beyond Buellton in that direction had been stopped. The officer told them the electronic signs north of the Rt. 154 junction were directing all non-local traffic to take the San Marcos Pass to Santa Barbara. Larger trucks had the choice to turn around and find a much longer route or curl up in a motel room until a lane or two could be opened through the gap.

They drove on south toward Las Cruces. The empty freeway was eerie. It felt more like an airstrip than a highway. Eagle Feather's plan was to find a place to park along the shoulder north of the Route 1 intersection and walk up the slope to the ridge that guarded the Las Cruces Valley. According to his map, the oil pipeline ascended this ridgeline on its way north. Since the proposed pipeline was to follow the old pipeline they should find some location signs.

They did. The big white sign near the top of the ridge was hard to miss with red letters saying DANGER across the top followed by the words HIGH PRESSURE PIPELINE. Glancing down the slope, Zack spotted another sign glinting in high chaparral. He hitched his pack higher on his shoulders. "Let's go."

The slope was gentle and except for clumps of sage and coyote bush here and there it was a grassy meadow with deer trails woven through it. They approached the second sign as close as possible avoiding contact with the poison oak clustered at its base. From here, they could look down the valley into some of the gap area and see the devastation the rifleman had wrought.

"Could simply have been a pipe blowout, I suppose," Zack said, musing.

Eagle Feather glanced at him. "It also could have been an enormous ground squirrel, White Man, but we both know it was not."

The destruction was on the level of a modern battlefield. Zack saw car hulks and something like a parcel truck on what remained of the road surface, all blackened from flames. Once the victims were removed, the firemen had not bothered to hose down the burning cars, their priority then to prevent wildfire spreading north and east into the wider spaces where control of the blaze would become far more difficult. They had managed it somehow by heroic effort. Smoke still curled up from hot embers here and there on the hillside. The fire that had climbed the walls on both sides of the gorge apparently was out. Zack could see the yellow suited firemen here and there on the steep slope putting out hotspots. Everything had an red-orange tint to it from the massive amount of flame retardant dropped by planes.

The two men stood in awe for several minutes overwhelmed, their eyes picking out details here and there, their minds struggling to comprehend the disaster. Eagle Feather broke his trance first and lifted his compass. He aligned it with his prepared map and sighted along it.

"The pipeline swings west here and then crosses under Route 1. This way."

His direction took them down the west side of the ridge into the Las Cruces Valley. They encountered a fence almost immediately.

"Keep your badge handy, White Man. We may piss off some landowners."

Zack grunted. "I'm keeping my pistol just as handy," he said, patting the SIG Saur 226 in its shoulder holster. "Out here, after that"––he waved toward the gorge—"guys are likely to shoot first and ask questions later."

He held the barbed wire spaced apart for Eagle Feather to climb through. "You have your weapon?" he asked, cocking an eyebrow at his friend.

Eagle Feather slid through, stood, and gave a slight smile. "I have what I need."

They descended to the valley floor, walked across a dusty dirt road and entered some brush bordering the creek. They had not yet found the next sign.

"I suppose on certain private properties they might not have signs," Zack suggested.

"That may be so, or they might not keep them at standard intervals." Eagle Feather rechecked the heading and scrambled down the bank into the mostly dry creek bed. An open swath through the brambles on the far bank suggested they were on the right path.

The compass steered them up a gradual rise and near the top they found another sign. Below them the usually busy Route 1 was completely empty.

"This should be where the pipeline swings south and crosses the road," Eagle Feather said, studying the map.

"If we walk up the road to that turnoff, it will make life easier," Zack said, his eyes on the thick brush that lined a creek bed on the far side of the highway.

Eagle Feather shook his head. "If we do not find something to fix the compass point on for our next bearing, we will be off course. Then we will have to come back here and do it all over again. That would not be easier."

Zack sighed, humped his pack higher on his back and followed Eagle Feather down the slope.

After crossing the empty road, they skidded down a loose shale slope through needle-like agave to an old dirt road surface. Crossing it, they came to a dry creek bed and again found signs where vegetation had been removed at one time.

Eagle Feather grunted in satisfaction. "This must be it." He checked his map, looked up the slope. "From here it angles slightly westward under that escarpment until it reaches the top of the ridge."

After the creek bed the terrain was forested and heavily pocked with thick brush. Their visibility was limited, it was necessary to take compass readings at more frequent intervals. This was real bushwhacking now, the vegetation thick underfoot. When a sinister rattle sounded somewhere in the undergrowth, Eagle Feather stopped.

"Your turn to the lead for a while, White Man," he said.

The lower reaches of the forested slope continued to be almost impenetrable. It was very slow going. It was another half hour before Zack stepped out of tall thicket into a wide meadow area. Above them he saw the next white sign.

"Bingo!"

"And there's another," Eagle Feather said, pointing. It glinted far beyond the first sign at the edge of a grove of wide-spreading oak trees near the ridge top.

No compass reading was needed now. They found heifer and deer paths to take them where they needed to go comfortably. The oak grove was in a saddle at the ridge crest, wide and level. The great outstretched limbs shaded the area beneath so that nothing grew but lush green grass. It was like an English country estate.

They walked comfortably beneath the great branches. Here and there monster boulders lay scattered about, some orange with lichens, others moss covered, some split with flat edges creating cave-like nooks and crannies. These great sarsens gave the appearance of a gateway, as if to a palace courtyard. Everywhere underfoot the grass was soft and spongy, the soil black and rich. Birds chirped and chattered in the branches above them. Spanish moss hung about like ornamental lace.

Zack touched Eagle Feather's arm to stop him. "Where are we now? Show me on your map."

The men found a table-sized boulder and settled on it, placing Eagle Feather's map between them. Zack glanced at it, then looked around them.

"The pipeline seems to be on a southwest heading here for a long run."

Eagle Feather placed the compass on the map. "Yes." He pointed. "That way."

Zack looked. He stood, looked again. "This oak forest seems to trend more to the west from here."

"Do you wish to follow the pipeline or follow the forest?"

Zack sat back down, put his forefinger on the map. "We need to follow the pipeline, but we also need to look for something hidden away from view. Over there"—he pointed along the compass heading—"is the ridgeline. I can see from here it is largely barren. You couldn't hide anything in that direction. But we need to remember the new pipeline will claim a wide swath of land, maybe as much as a mile in places."

"And that could include this forest area."

Zack nodded. "Right. This vale looks much more promising."

Eagle Feather nodded and folded up the map. "Lead on, White Man."

CHAPTER TWENTY-ONE

Zack led the way among the boulders under the oak canopy. The ground sloped away gradually now and he caught glimpses of a valley far below. They came to a roadway, little more than a hiking path at right angles to their direction. Beyond it the brush was thick and the green leaves suspiciously shiny.

"Not going in there," Zack said. He turned right and followed the lane west. The way was covered in tall grasses, narrow and little used. The barrier of impenetrable thicket continued on the downslope side. The road turned up a small hill and around a bend.

A fence barred their way. It was a four strand barbed wire fence, sagging in places, held up by old dry wood posts. But the gate across the path had been reinforced with a steel post on each side. A thick, shiny gold lock secured the gate mechanism.

They stood for a moment and studied it.

"Maybe now is the time to try your new set of keys," Eagle Feather said.

Zack nodded and fished in his pocket. He looked at the two keys in his palm, looked at the lock and selected one. It fit. The lock snapped open and Zack pushed the gate wide.

"Whoever this is seems a little too eager for us to join him," Zack said. He slid a hand under his jacket and loosed the latch on his holster, then glanced at Eagle Feather. "Ready?"

Eagle Feather motioned him ahead. "After you, White Man."

Beyond the gate, the roadway, still really a path, swung down the slope and reentered the oak forest. Here it widened, the emerald grass reappeared. The ancient oak canopy with trailing Spanish moss overhead reminded Zack of a southern plantation. The path beneath their feet turned to gravel. There were signs of human habitation—a picnic table at the base of a great old oak, a wood swing suspended from the limb of another. Off to one side there was a mound of fresh dirt and a small stone slab.

The old growth oak forest sloped gently down toward the valley nestled in a cañada gentled by erosion in the ancient past while leaving enough of a protective wall for larger trees to thrive. Zack guessed there must be a spring somewhere nearby.

The two men walked a few feet apart, wary but curious. The huge oaks were thick through here, the road winding like a Victorian carriageway among them. It felt like a memorial park to Zack. Then came a glint of reddish brown and a small barn took shape through the trees. The sound of chickens and guinea fowl came to their ears. A goat called to them from somewhere inside the enclosure.

Near it stood the house. They approached it from the rear. The walls were of natural wood planking horizontally overlaid like roofing with a framed rear door and several windows trimmed in green to match the emerald lawn surrounding it. It was wide, built ranch style with a single story and a shake roof. Flower beds surrounded it, the plantings tastefully selected and placed.

They followed a drive around to the front. Here was a porch the width of the house with a hand-hewn natural wood railing, its floor painted white. Three rockers with thick cushions and a small tea table were to one side of the front door. In the doorway itself a woman and watched them approach.

"Who are you? Are you with the oil company?" she asked. Her voice had a tremor. Her eyes were lined with anxiety.

Zack reached for his credential wallet. "No, ma'am. We are with the Federal Bureau of Investigation." He held up his badge. "May we speak with you?"

She appeared to be in her forties, Zack judged, although her face was etched with worry. Despite that, she was a handsome woman.

"My husband is away just now," she said. "Can you come back another time?"

Zack tried his gentlest smile. "I'm afraid this can't wait, ma'am. May we come in?"

She stood as if frozen for a moment, then sighed. Her shoulders drooped and she stood aside for them to enter.

They came into a large living area that extended the depth of the house with a large window facing the barn and the tree groves beyond. A couch and several confortable chairs were tastefully arranged on a woven carpet of Mexican design. She waved them to a seat, then perched tenuously on the edge of another.

"Is there a problem?" she asked. She looked from one to the other.

"May I know your name, please?" Zack asked.

"I am Irma Jean Dench," she said.

"And your husband?"

"My husband's name is William Dench."

Zack passed his credentials to her. "As you see, I am Agent Zack Tolliver and this is my associate, Eagle Feather."

Irma Jean looked at the Navajo curiously.

'How do?" Eagle Feather said, unsmiling.

She nodded, looked back at Zack and waited.

"Where were you last night, Mrs. Dench?" Zack asked.

"Right here."

"And your husband?"

She hesitated a moment. "He was here with me."

"You must have been aware of a very large explosion last evening right around five p.m."

She nodded, her eyes looked frightened. "Yes." It was almost a whisper.

"And your husband must have heard it too. What did he think it was?"

She looked down. "He didn't say."

Zack studied her. A tear had formed in the corner of her eye.

"He wasn't here, was he," Zack said softly.

Irma Jean started to protest, but couldn't sustain it. Finally, she simply shook her head.

"Do you know where he was?"

"No." Again, barely a whisper.

"When did you last see him, please?" Zack asked.

"He was in the barn most of the morning after breakfast yesterday. He came in for lunch. I think he left after that. I expected he might be home for dinner, but he didn't come back. I haven't seen him since." Another tear edged out the first.

"So you know nothing of his whereabouts since noon or so yesterday."

She nodded, then asked, "Agent Tolliver, is my husband in some kind of trouble?"

"Mrs. Dench, the loud noise you heard yesterday evening was a gas explosion. A high pressure gas pipeline in the gap ruptured. We believe it was sabotage."

"And you think—Bill—?"

Zack reached into his pocket and took out the two keys. He passed them to Irma Jean. "Do you recognize these?"

She looked at them, her eyes flicked up to Zack's face. "This looks like the gate key. And this...this looks like the barn key." Her eyes held his, questioning.

"Those keys were in an envelope that was placed in my hotel room," Zack said. "Can you think of anyone who might have done that?"

Irma Jean gasped, looked again at the keys in her palm. "Why, no one but Bill had these keys—and me, of course. Bill must..." She stopped in confusion. "But why would he do such a thing?"

Zack leaned close from his chair. "This is difficult, Mrs. Dench, but we believe your husband has some sort of agenda with the oil companies using pipelines through Gaviota Pass. Whatever it is, he wants it known."

Irma Jean lowered her head. A tear fell. "I've been afraid of something like this," she said, her voice timorous. "He has been so upset ever since the pipeline representative came here to tell us we may have to move."

Zack glanced at Eagle Feather, then asked, "Why would you have to move?"

Irma Jean's lips tightened. "Bill told me—after all these years!—we don't even own the land our house"—she waved an arm—"our entire farm sits on. We built it over the years, just the two of us to be completely self sufficient. But how could we be if we didn't even own the land?" She began to sob. "The man told us we might have to move, depending upon the final decision on the pipeline route. Bill kept saying not to worry"—another sob—"and then my mother died, but Bill wouldn't let me bury her at the church. He didn't want to call attention to us." She sobbed louder. "Now I know why." She gave herself a minute. "So we spread her ashes here and Bill kept saying he would never let anyone disturb her. No one would bulldoze her up." Her eyes bore into Zack's. "You think it was him, don't you? You think that's how he planned to stop them. You think he blew up the pipeline!"

Zack held her gaze. "Yes, Mrs. Dench, we believe that is the case. That is why we are here. Mrs. Dench, we need you to help us find him before anyone else is hurt."

She gave him a flustered look. "I have no idea where he could be. He comes and goes, I never know where."

"Does he go to bars, or belong to the Y—anything like that?"

She shook her head. "No, he'd never go where there are people. He is solitary, he loves the woods. Except to shop for things he can't make himself, I don't think he ever leaves the woods." She gave another little sob. "Lately, he's either been away someplace or in the barn."

Zack looked at Eagle Feather. They both rose. "I think it's time we looked in the barn, Mrs. Dench. Would you take us there, please?"

They crossed the long green sward to the big barn doors. The breeze whispered through the oaks, rattling the brittle leaves and waving the Spanish moss. The sun dappled the side of the barn with light and dark puzzle pieces. The smell of fresh rich earth was in the air.

Zack understood why a man would want to live here and would give his entire being to protect the place from destruction. But how had he come to be here without buying the land? Why had he lied to his wife all these years?

The hasp on the barn door lock came free with a well oiled click when Irma Jean turned the key. Zack took the key back from her. It would be evidence.

The big doors creaked open. As his eyes adjusted, Zack saw a typical barn with hay scattered about the floor, a loft extending half the length of the building, several stalls with smaller exits behind, probably to the barnyard for the various animals to move freely. He'd heard the chickens and guinea fowl and goat, now he heard the grunt of a pig. The couple had raised the creatures they needed to provide food, clothing, dairy, eggs and much more. There were cultivating tools, including a plow. A harness hung on the wall. Zack guessed Bill had an animal to pull the plow, maybe a mule. Everything was self sustaining.

He turned to Irma Jean. "The electric—?"

She pointed. "There's a rise that way. We have a wind turbine there, just a small one, but it's all we need. And we have solar in the clearing."

Zack nodded his admiration. These people were well and truly off the grid.

Eagle Feather motioned for Zack's attention. He was looking at a small door built into the wall near one of the stalls. There was a padlock on it.

"Where does this lead, Mrs. Dench?" Zack asked.

"That is the stairway to the basement. Bill's workshop is down there, but I don't have a key."

"With your permission, Mrs. Dench, we'll remove the hasp." At her nod, Eagle Feather brought a penknife from his pocket and used a Philips head tool to remove the hasp. He opened the door and switched on the light. Like everything else they had seen so far, the stairwell was clean and well lit, the items on the shelves along it very orderly.

The stairway was short and brought them to a hard-packed earthen floor and a small room. The walls were whitewashed. There were no shelves, but wine barrels filled with a variety of items lined the walls. Behind and under the stairway was a large work bench. Zack found a switch and turned on the work light.

Eagle Feather turned to Irma Jean, hovering behind them. "Your husband has a rifle."

She nodded.

"It is not here."

She nodded again.

Eagle Feather rubbed a finger on the work bench surface, smelled it. "Gun powder." He pointed to a reload press attached to the edge of the bench. "He loads his own." A Ziploc bag of shiny bullets nearby confirmed this. He opened the large central drawer. Inside was a set of calipers in a felt box, a small scale, a large blue case tumbler, an ultrasound cleaner, a box of shell casings, a funnel and various tools such as tweezers. On top of the bench in a neat group on the far side was a box of primers, a jar of powder, a can of case lubrication and two empty rifle cartridges.

Zack glanced at the bullets and casings. "Winchester .308," he said. "And those"—he pointed to a bag near the back of the drawer— "are incendiary bullets."
He looked at Irma Jean. "I'm afraid your husband has been a very bad boy."

Eagle Feather was peering into the various barrels. He reached into one and pulled out several burlap bags. Still holding them, he peered in other barrels. "This is not good," he said.

Zack's head jerked up to look at him. "What's not good?"

"I believe he has buried caches." He went from barrel to barrel. "He has food, water, tools, clothing, even shoes." Eagle Feather looked at Zack. "This man intends to stay on the run for a very long time."

CHAPTER TWENTY-TWO

Irma Jean was clearly devastated. Her life was crumbling around her. She must be realizing she might never see her husband again. Her home would be taken away. She had lived so long in isolation she had nowhere to go and no one else to turn to. Could any situation be more hopeless?

Zack felt her thoughts. He walked with her back to the house from the barn, stayed close, guided her by her elbow. At the house he saw her seated and began to brew some tea. He'd left Eagle Feather in the barn to glean what he could from anything he found there. Shortly their hunt for Bill Dench would begin.

Zack had already notified the county sheriff and their work had already begun, but he doubted they'd have much luck. Bill was obviously creative and a woodsman and had evidently been planning this a long, long time.

"Mrs. Dench, I've called my associate, Agent James McLeish. He is on his way to be with you. He'll stay here with you until we've found your husband."

Zack was standing at the stove in the kitchen. She sat in her chair in the living room and stared at him. Her eyes were blank, her face drawn.

"I don't need protection from my husband."

"No, ma'am, but he needs protection from us. In a situation like this the police are on edge, justifiably ready to protect themselves. It is possible your husband may try to come home. James McLeish is an experienced agent and will know what to do. And you, ma'am, would be the most important part of that situation."

Zack glanced at her. She was nodding but her head was down, her shoulders caved in, a figure of abject misery. He prattled on, hoping to distract her with details. "A police matron will be with James. He tells me she's a warm, wonderful woman who will keep you company for a while." He glanced at her again. "How long has it been since you've had female company?"

She did not respond, but he saw the sigh escape her.

The tea kettle whistled and Zack rescued it. Next came the comforting sound of hot water on the tea bag and the aroma of spice. "Then there's the animals," Zack said. "They need attention and Agent McLeish will help you with that." Zack picked up the cup and saucer and walked into the living room chuckling. "But you'll need to guide him with that. He's pretty much a city boy."

Eagle Feather appeared at the outer doorway. He had a pack on his shoulders and held another in his hand.

Zack handed Irma Jean the tea. She balanced it on a knee and sipped it with an automatic motion. Zack gestured toward Eagle Feather. "I'll be just out on the porch with my friend. Please think about where Bill might have gone. We can keep him safe if we have enough information." He patted her hand and stepped outside to join Eagle Feather. He glanced at him. "Thoughts?"

Eagle Feather took his map from his pocket and held it on the porch rail. "We know where he had to be to shoot the pipeline. That places him east of the gap. After the explosion there would be no way to get back to this side of the canyon, with the fire, airdrops, and all. So we'd assume he heads east along the Santa Ynez range. In these last twenty hours he could already be beyond Lake Cachuma and deep into the back country of the San Rafael Mountains and the Sierra Madre. He will be very hard to find in all that territory."

"His plan seems perfect," Zack said. "No one knew to look for him until now, which gives him all the time he needs to get beyond the more populated areas along the Santa Ynez Mountain ridges overnight. Then he just disappears."

Eagle Feather eyed Zack. "His wife knows nothing?"

"It seems not. She is clearly shattered. Until recently, she thought they owned this land. I guess Bill's been keeping a lot of secrets."

"What will happen to her?"

"She's not guilty of anything I can think of. But she's pretty broken up. She'll have to find a way to start over." He cocked an ear. "I think we have company."

The faraway chainsaw-like sound of ATVs floated up from the valley. Soon two quads and a white pickup truck came up the driveway. The pickup's front doors flopped open, McLeish climbed down from the driver's side and a woman in uniform came from the passenger side.

McLeish walked up to Zack and Eagle Feather. "So you say this is our man and he's loose."

"That's about the size of it."

Zack explained his plan. "Mrs. Dench is extremely upset, as you might imagine. She's gonna need a lot of care and understanding, but we want her to be here if at all possible in case Bill comes home. Her safety comes first, obviously, but..."

McLeish nodded. "Gotcha. I've been talking to Susan here on the way up. Can't do better than her, I think."

Zack took Susan and McLeish inside and introduced them to Irma Jean.

Susan immediately sat on the couch beside the devastated woman and placed an arm around her. "Oh, you poor dear!"

As the women began to talk, Zack and McLeish ducked back outside. Zack pointed to the ATVs and the agents standing nearby, waiting for instructions.

"You'll need to hide those things, get rid of the tracks. There's room in the barn." He scratched his head. "Eagle Feather went through everything in that building pretty thoroughly, but I'd still have these guys take another hard look. We really have no idea where this guy went other than the fact he's supplied himself in advance." He grimaced at McLeish. "He's going to be harder to dig out than a porcupine in a gopher hole." He started to walk away, had one more thought. "And there's always the chance he didn't go anywhere. Don't be a target." He had another thought. "Actually, you only need to hide one of those quads. Eagle Feather and I will take the other."

Zack stood next to the ATV and chatted briefly with an agent whom he knew slightly while Eagle Feather loaded up the small vehicle with their packs and some food supplies and water he'd taken from the barn cellar.

McLeish came striding over before they climbed aboard. He was waving a rifle. "You're gonna need this unless you want to play that ducks in a shooting gallery game."

Zack took it with a sheepish grin and secured it under some strapping. "Guess we're being a little over confident here."

"Listen, I just heard from the troopers. Apparently Bill Dench owns a white Ford 250 pickup truck, registration and license all up to date. They just found it abandoned at the north bound rest area south of the tunnel."

Zack nodded his thanks. "I guess he's off on foot in the mountains, like Eagle Feather thought."

Eagle Feather was ready to be off. He sat at the wheel, impatiently watching Zack and McLeish exchange their final words. "You are like two drunks with one bottle. It is time to go."

As they bounced down the drive in a dust cloud, Zack glanced at the Navajo. "Got any idea where you're going?"

Eagle Feather reached a hand over and pulled a map from a compartment between them. "We're on the track that leads to Agua Caliente Road. It will take us to Hollister Ranch Road next to the Pacific Ocean. From there we can access the freeway south of the gap. We can decide where to go from there."

"Sounds good to me." Zack leaned back in the seat, stretched his feet out and relaxed best he could as the quad bounced its way down the mountainside. On Agua Caliente Road they passed impressive gates to large homes. Fruit orchards and vineyards perched here and there on the slopes. The valley leveled as it opened toward the shore. Eagle Feather did not need the map and turned at each divide with confidence. Then the Pacific came into view, its far reaches obscured by the inevitable fog. Closer at hand, the water sparkled in the sun.

Eagle Feather turned left heading east on Hollister Ranch Road. The road dipped and turned as it followed the features of the shoreline, always reemerging with the glistening ocean water on their right. A sharp curve and a steep descent brought them to the Gaviota Beach State Park and campground complex and a gatekeeper's booth. The campground appeared full of trailers and vans bearing news communication logos.

They drove along the camp ground entrance road to the freeway. It was empty. A barricade blocked the freeway north of them. CHP officers were waiting in their patrol cars to intercept all traffic. They merely glanced at the small ATV as it turned away and headed south on the freeway.

"So where now?" Zack asked, looking back over his shoulder at the gap entrance.

Eagle Feather waved a hand to his left. "There's an area just up ahead on the slope where there used to be a hotel. There's nothing there now except access roads. We can stop there where there is a view and make our plan."

He took the overpass at Mariposa Reina and made an immediate left and a right and left again onto a deserted roadway. It brought them across a long field to another deserted paved road and then up a steep slope. Eagle Feather finally stopped the little vehicle at a turnaround with a wide open view across the frontal slopes of the Santa Ynez range.

"He's up in there somewhere," Eagle Feather said, pointing.

Zack looked across the vast land, the Pacific Ocean on one side, shimmering here, dark there with layers of fog, and on the other side the rugged bare peaks. In the middle was the coastal plain, green and patched with pastures and slashed by arroyos.

"The only way to find him is to track him," Zack said.

Eagle Feather nodded, his eyes on the far peaks. "To do that we must cut his trail."

"We know where he had to be to shoot the gas pipeline. But after the blast, the fire, the air retardant dumps..." Zack hesitated, looked at Eagle Feather. "For all we know, he didn't make it."

"He made it. The blast, the fire—it was all part of his plan." Eagle Feather stared along the ridge leading to a peak on their left. "The terrain from where he took his shot the last time was all open ground above and behind him up to the Tunnel View Trail, the trail you came along. But after he took the shot, he must have run uphill like a mule deer to beat the blast."

"Maybe the initial blast wasn't as bad as it appeared."

Eagle Feather looked a question at Zack.

Zack shrugged. "I understood the internal pressure of the gas pipe was around two hundred pounds per square inch. A ruptured Alaskan pipeline that was pressured at eight hundred pounds per square inch sent a flume of oil a quarter mile. A gas jet would probably disperse sooner and the pressure in this pipe was a quarter of the Alaskan one, so at a guess guess the jet might have gone two or three hundred feet at the most initially. That would take it across the highway and maybe a little bit up the eastern slope. The pipe is steel, the integrity of the metal around the hole from the bullet might hold out for a while and the jet spray thus remain relatively focused, although tailing upward at its end. It's the ignition and explosion that rips the pipe open. When that happens the distance lessens and the spray widens into more of an upward direction, away from the eastern wall." Zack glanced at Eagle Feather, who was grinning. "Okay, okay, you see where I'm going. There are two key factors here—how long was it before ignition, and how far did the initial fireball actually travel horizontally? Maybe he didn't have to be all that far up the slope to escape."

"Once a fire got started it would move up that wall fast," Eagle Feather said.

"Yes, it would. And that brings us to my first point. When did the gas actually ignite? We can't assume the gas automatically ignited when the bullet entered."

Eagle Feather stared at Zack. "There might have been a time delay."

"Exactly."

"He must have known," Eagle Feather said. "That is why he had the incendiary bullets."

Zack nodded. "Yes. He could time the explosion to his advantage if it didn't happen immediately. I think we need to start our search at the scene. Once we determine the sequence of the explosion, we will have a better idea how to deal with it."

Eagle Feather turned and walked toward the ATV. "The sooner we start, the sooner we find him."

CHAPTER TWENTY-THREE

The full realization of the size of the tragedy about to implode her life came to Irma Jean by degrees. She knew Bill to be a determined man, a brave man, a man not likely to be pushed or bullied. She saw him as principled and highly moralistic. Yes, he was unconventional, a trait many people automatically condemned, but to Irma Jean it was the natural outcome of true moral fiber and integrity. Others talked about what was good for the world; Bill did something about it.

But not this way. Bill would never risk lives. He was all about preserving lives. Irma Jean could not comprehend how Bill could be responsible for an explosion and fire that hurt innocent people randomly. How would he have thought this action was a means to preserve their lives here when it must so obviously end it all? To blame Bill for this was to say he was a dangerous radical, ready to throw everything he loved away just to make his point. But that was not him, that was not her Bill.

Unless something had changed him dramatically in the last few years, that is. She remembered his reaction to the pipeline rupture and the subsequent damage to the coastline and its animal life. He was beyond chagrinned. But he didn't react with anger, he didn't shout about it and protest and carry a placard and march. Instead, he took towels and cleaners and whatever he could find to the beach and rescued sea birds and cleaned stones and sifted sand and did what he could for long hours, day after day. He was all about the environment––he wouldn't blow it up.

And yet—all the evidence in the barn, the rifle shells, the supplies meant for caches to hide away from the law, his secretive ways—did she really know what he had been about?

Susan Colleen, the matron from the sheriff's department, had been very helpful. She reminded Irma Jean to focus on herself, take care of herself, have faith that things would work out, remember that this would pass. One step at a time, she would say. Just one step at a time.

Irma Jean was sipping her tea and listening to Susan when Agent McLeish entered the kitchen. She like James. He was a nice, friendly man, a big huggy Teddy bear type who seemed sincerely concerned with helping her through this. He took a seat at the table with them.

"And how are my two favorite ladies doing?"

They both smiled.

McLeish looked at Irma Jean. "Mrs. Dench, I need to ask you one or two more questions if you don't mind."

Irma Jean looked at him, quietly nodded. One step at a time.

McLeish rested his chin on his elbows and leaned in toward her. "I don't know how much Agent Tolliver was able to tell you before he left. You know we are worried Bill had something to do with the pipeline rupture last night. You know he had the self-loaded rifle bullets capable of penetrating the pipeline. You may not know he had incendiary loads also, bullets you don't use for hunting but that would certainly facilitate the explosion of gas."

As the agent spoke, Irma felt a tear form and quickly wiped it away. She felt Susan's warm hand wrap over her own on the table.

McLeish cleared his throat. "Well, what I needed to ask about was those barrels in the cellar. Do you know how your husband obtained them?"

Irma Jean nodded. "We know wine makers in the area. I'm sure he got them from them."

"Were you here when they arrived, ma'am?"

Irma Jean thought about it, remembering. "Yes, I remember because he had to assemble the staves and hoops in the yard before he took them into the cellar."

"What did he tell you they were for?"

"Storage. He didn't want shelves. The barrels were free, he said, and would work better for him."

She watched McLeish. He seemed to struggle with the next words.

"Mrs. Dench, are you aware of the murder we've been investigating, the woman who was apparently burned to death in the gap several days ago?"

She shuddered. "Yes, that was terrible."

"Well, you should know the woman's body was surrounded by several hoops, hoops from wine barrels just like those in your barn cellar."

Irma Jean felt an urge to throw up. This was all just horrible beyond imagining. "You think—do you really think my husband capable of something like that?"

Agent McLeish shook his head sadly. "I have no way of knowing, Mrs. Dench. I don't know your husband. But I feel it is important for you to know all that is going on. With some luck, we'll find your husband and he will explain everything." He stood. "That's why it's important you tell us anything you can remember." He gave a sad smile and left.

A horrible thought flashed into Irma Jean's mind. She remembered Bill's set jaw when he promised her no one would ever bulldoze up her mother. She never asked how he had cremated her, she didn't want to know. She had been very angry with him then. But he'd given her the ashes in a lovely container and they'd worked out the service together and scattered her ashes as she had wanted. It had seemed so right.

But now—she almost choked on the thought. Could the woman they found burned in the gap...? They never identified her, did they? And now the agent asked about the wine barrels, the hoops? When had Bill gotten those barrels? Was it before she heard about the woman in the gap? News came so slow to her here, it was just hard to know. Could Bill have done that to her mother? She gave a gasp, felt Susan's arm tighten on her shoulders. No, he loved her as much as she did. He wouldn't, he couldn't have done that. But if he did burn her there, what ashes did he give her to scatter? Were they from some animal? She shuddered.

Irma Jean made a conscious decision not to believe what her mind was describing to her. It was too horrible to contemplate. Bill could never have done these things, he hadn't done them and that was all there was to it. When Bill was back home safe and sound they'd all learn the truth.

Most important for now was Bill's safe return. She would help with that every way she could. He had to come home safe. After that, everything would be resolved. One step at a time.

CHAPTER TWENTY-FOUR

While Eagle Feather drove at bone rattling speed down the ridge of the slope and onto the empty freeway, Zack held on with braced feet and called the sheriff's office. They connected him to the event commander. Zack explained his mission.

"You'll want to meet Jack Fuergeson. He's on the slope now. Hang on, I'll see if he can spare a moment." The line buzzed and held and in another minute the man was back. "Sure, yeah, he says meet him a half mile north of the tunnel. He'll be in a Caltrans truck."

They showed their credentials to the officer guarding the blockaded freeway and raced on through the tunnel, eerily quiet now but for the roar of their own two cycle engine. Beyond the tunnel they saw the first evidence of fire damage on the western slope. It seemed extensive to their view, green oak leaves browned and twisted, charred undergrowth, lots of debris. Threads of smoke still worked upward here and there. As they came around the corner toward the north they encountered the first of several car hulks askew and still smoldering on the roadway. Both sides of the road showed the effects of intense heat and blast. A crater formed by the force of the explosion had eaten into the southbound roadway across the first traffic lane. A car hulk was precariously balanced at its edge. Zack spotted the white Caltrans pickup and pointed it out to Eagle Feather who worked the ATV toward the right shoulder around another burnt auto. They pulled up behind the truck and stepped out.

Zack saw they were at the epicenter of the blast. The original pipeline would have been directly opposite them across the freeway and slightly upslope. That area was blasted away entirely and a large chunk of pipe lay on the roadway opposite them. In one place the pavement had been peeled back like a carpet.

A man approached from the truck cab with an outstretched hand. "Hi, I'm Jack Fuergeson. Which of you is Zack Tolliver?"

Zack grabbed his hand. "That's me. Thanks for agreeing to see us. This is my colleague Eagle Feather."

Eagle Feather shook his hand. Jack was a stocky man with thick wiry eyebrows over penetrating blue eyes sunk in a genial face. He pointed up the slope. "I've got a body for you," he said.

Zack caught his breath, glanced at Eagle Feather who stared at Fuergeson.

"You said a body—up there?"

"Yeah, that's right. Just found him an hour ago kinda behind some rocks. Couldn't figure it out, guessed it must be some poor unlucky bastard of a hiker. But after talkin' to you, maybe we got your perp."

Zack looked at Eagle Feather, back to Jack. "Sheriff's office?"

"They got a team on the way. A highway patrolman is guarding the body now. Nothings been moved."

Eagle Feather stared up the slope. "You find anything else up there?"

Jack studied Eagle Feather, looked up the slope himself. "If you mean any other bodies, no. The victim looked to be by himself. But you can see"—he waved at the tangle of burnt undergrowth, fallen trees and limbs, scorched and exploded rocks—"that doesn't mean we didn't miss something."

"Can you take us to the body?" Zack asked.

Fuergeson nodded, stepped to the back of the truck and opened a metal door. He pulled out fireman boots and gave a pair to each of them. "You're going to need those." He reached in for a pair of helmets with masks attached. "And these."

Jack armed himself with a small axe and walked across the shoulder up the steep highway cut, slipping some, digging into the wet soil where he could. Zack found the boots exceedingly clumsy but was glad to have them when he encountered the mud, water pools and piles of debris.

"I'm steering wide of these overgrown places," Jack explained. "That poison oak is a bitch, even when burned."

146

Once beyond the highway cut the slope angle decreased and they were climbing through tall spindly burnt trees into a meadow. The large boulders here and there looked familiar, but the fire had changed the appearance of the place dramatically.

Eagle Feather grunted. "That is where we found the cartridge," he said to Zack, nodding that way.

The Navajo was right. Far up the slope loomed the enormous boulders from which the ghostly forms had emerged. He felt a sudden shiver as he remembered. If the figures had been an omen, it was being fulfilled.

There was a shout from above. Jack waved to someone. They climbed the last yards to a large rock. Zack realized the stone appeared even larger because the undergrowth surrounding had been reduced by fire. Behind it lay a dark figure. He could see only the feet from here, see a leather boot sole flapped loose exposing a blackened foot.

He approached closer and saw the figure of a man tucked into a fetal position behind the rock. He must have had just time enough to assume that position before the fire roared over him. All his outer layers were burnt down to the skin. His left arm and hand lay across his face and head. His hair, worn long, was matted, wet and scorched. Smears of orange retardant flecked across him and over the rock.

"No rifle," Eagle Feather said.

The patrolman came to stand with the men. "We've not moved him or searched him yet."

Zack showed the man his credentials. "We'll be taking over here. He's a suspect in our case."

The policeman smiled. "The deputies will be happy. They were looking at long nights, otherwise."

Zack was staring at the matt of hair, orange-red streaked, damp and covered by ash. He reached down and pulled the victim's arm away. The face was surprisingly untouched revealing a man about forty, clean shaven, attractive if it wasn't for the large exit wound at the hairline.

The patrolman gave a gasp. Zack dropped the arm back into place.

"This man was shot from behind before the fire, arranged behind this rock," Zack said. He reached in his own pocket and brought out a small photo, passed it to Eagle Feather. "Looks to me like we found Bill Dench, and he didn't do it."

"Didn't do what?" Fuergeson asked.

"He didn't shoot the pipeline. He was dead when that happened."

Fuergeson studied Zack. "Shooting the pipeline wouldn't necessarily cause the explosion. He might have shot it, thrown away the gun, and started to run, making it just this far. He—"

Zack was shaking his head. "He didn't shoot himself. Whoever shot him didn't shoot him here." Zack pulled up the man's arm again. "Look at the rock surface opposite his head along the line of the entry and exit wound. There is no impact mark on that rock." He shook his head again. "Someone shot him from behind, dragged or carried him here, arranged him, then shot the pipeline. After that, he might have had a few seconds to move away up the slope, reload with an incendiary bullet, and set off the explosion."

Eagle Feather was already moving up the slope.

Zack watched him. "I think my friend Eagle Feather will find the place he sheltered to reload and shoot the bullets to set off the explosion. Our hunt will begin there." He turned to the patrolman. "When the deputies arrive, make sure they know we are investigating a murder. I'll be in touch with the sheriff."

Zack turned to Fuergeson and shook his hand. "Thanks for your help. We'll get your boots and helmets back to you. If you find anything else, like, say, a half-burnt discarded rifle, let us know." He passed him his card, grinned, and moved up the slope after Eagle Feather.

The Navajo had paused just below a small grove of oak trees surrounded by a loose necklace grouping of small boulders. The fire damage here wasn't as heavy, although retardant had been dropped in greater quantities. The firefighters had chosen this place to halt the fire's advance. Farther upslope there was less fire damage.

Eagle Feather was on his knees studying an area where a boulder leaned into a thick tree trunk. A cavity had formed there, a good place to avoid the blast. The Navajo dug through the leaves in the cranny, which was remarkably untouched by either fire or flame retardant. After a minute or so his expression changed and he brought his hand out. In his fingers was a shell casing. He sniffed it. "Incendiary."

Zack took it, bounced it in his palm. "He planned well. First he shot Bill from behind, maybe with his own rifle. Then he hauled the body where we found it. When do you think he shot the pipeline?"

Eagle Feather stared down the slope to the damaged roadway. "It is a long shot from here, but not beyond the range of a good marksman. He may have needed just the one shot."

Zack looked at his friend. "So he could have shot it from up here using the incendiary bullet."

Eagle Feather nodded. "Nice and safe."

"Meanwhile hoping—expecting Bill's body would burn enough to cover up the murder and make it look as if he'd been hoisted by his own petard." At Eagle Feather's stare he explained. "Killed in his own attempt to do others harm. It's an old expression."

"Whatever you say, White Man."

"But what about the rifle? If we assume it was Bill's rifle, and we know he had one, why not leave it near him?"

"He could not do that and take the safe shot from up here. Once the explosion had occurred, he could not go back down without leaving traces or facing fire."

"Right." Zack picked up a stone, pitched it down the slope. "He might have tried to throw the rifle back down there, but it's pretty far and if he didn't throw it far enough, it would land uphill from Bill's body."

"And that would not make sense."

"Right. So, he had to take it with him. That's his vulnerability. If he is caught with it, he's the guilty party. He's going to have to dump it."

"But where? He can not dump it just anywhere. It is a hot potato." Eagle Feather glanced sideways at Zack. "That is an old expression that means—"

"Okay, okay, yes. But I get your point. If it was Bill's rifle, and it ended up anywhere above Bill's body, everyone will know Bill didn't shoot the pipeline. It either has to disappear completely, which would still leave suspicion in everyone's mind since he obviously needed a rifle to shoot the pipeline, or it has to be found at a later date somewhere near the body."

Eagle Feather nodded. "If it were me, that would be my choice."

"So he will come back."

"He will come back."

CHAPTER TWENTY-FIVE

They tried to pick up his trail, but the layers of fire retardant and big firemen boots along the paths during and after the fire made it a mishmash and even Eagle Feather's skilled eyes couldn't identify a useful footprint so they gave it up and trudged down to where they'd left the ATV. The Caltrans truck was still there even though Fuergeson wasn't so they left the boots and helmets next to the truck.

On the drive back to the Dench farm, Zack thought about what he knew and what it all meant. He did know they had a lot of questions for Irma Jean.

The lee of the hills was shadowy now, the sun lower in the west. A slight breeze had picked up and swirled dust on the dry ridge road as they climbed toward the farm. Zack was struck again by the farm's isolation, hidden away as it was in a valley no one might suspect was there. Bill had chosen well. But what else had entered into his choice? Was he related in some way to the Corliss couple, murdered in 1864? Did this piece of land once belong to them? Were Bill's actions related to that connection? Zack would have to ask Irma Jean these questions, but he knew it would be hard on the woman whether she knew the answers or not.

Zack had called ahead and one of the agents stood next to the unlocked gate and waved them through. The news of Bill's passing had been relayed to the matron to break to Irma Jean. The house was deathly still as they approached it.

McLeish stepped out on the porch as the ATV neared. Zack walked to him and nodded wordlessly. They both stared out at the fruit trees beginning to blend into each others' shadows in the deepening gloom.

"Tough on her," McLeish said.

"Got to be. How is she holding up?"

"Well enough so far."

Zack squared his shoulders. "Well, we have to speak to her. Time's short and there's still a long day ahead."

McLeish stepped aside and held the door for Zack to enter. He found Irma Jean on the couch leaning against Susan's shoulder, her eyes open and staring, her face still."

Zack moved a chair in front of her and sat down. He caught her eye.

"Bill didn't do this, you know."

She said nothing.

"He was part of it, but I don't think he really knew what "it" was." Zack saw her eye flicker, her gaze become more focused, and continued. "Someone else was steering his action and that someone killed him in the end. We need to find him."

"Bill put my mother's remains out in public view with those hoops like an exhibit for all to see."

"We don't know that yet."

"I know it."

"If he did, it was because someone else convinced him it was for a higher cause."

She partially sat up. "Everything to him was a higher cause—higher than me, higher than my m-m-mother!" She melted into sobs. "He lied to me so—many—times!"

Susan patted her arm. "I think everything he did was for you and this farm, for your lives together here."

Irma Jean shrugged her off, pointed at Zack. "Who is this man who held such control over Bill? My husband was very independent. People didn't tell him what to do."

"We don't know who he is, but we hope to find out tonight. We think he will return to the burn area to make one more attempt to incriminate your husband. This man is very manipulative. He would have seen your husband's distress over the pipeline situation and what it must mean to this valley, to him and to you and he would have played upon that, probably with ideas he'd twist to make Bill think he'd thought of them himself."

Irma Jean's face was scornful. "Bill was very independent and very bright. He'd never fall for that."

"It is easy to convince a man to choose a path he already wants to take," Eagle Feather said.

"And once he is started along that path, it is difficult to turn back and the choices become more complicated," McLeish said.

"You say Bill didn't burst that gas line, so why was he there?" Irma Jean asked. "And why did he load the bullets for his rifle with that fire starting stuff? It doesn't make sense."

Zack gave his head a slow shake. "There is a lot we don't know yet. But we can say with absolute certainty that Bill did not fire the shot that blew up the gas line." He glanced out the window. It was already dusk. "We need to go now to try to catch this man." He stood, looked gently down at her. "As soon as I have the answers to your questions, I will tell you."

He looked at McLeish. "You coming?"

McLeish grinned. "Wouldn't miss it."

They took McLeish's pickup this time. In the back were two scoped 721 Remington rifles with tripods and magazines of four rounds each. Each agent had his SIG Saur 9mm and personal weapon. Eagle Feather had whatever Eagle Feather had.

Zack sat in the middle of the wide bench-seat and opened a topo map on the vehicle's display of the south entrance to Gaviota Gap. He converted it to the window display where it appeared in three dimensions with red lines. He guided a pointer to the north end of the tunnel.

"I think if we approach through the tunnel without lights and park to the right just before the bend we won't be visible to anyone up the slope. We get equipped there, then walk along the roadway to where we can drop into this low area just beyond the cliffs. From there we cross an area of brush and should find a trail there." He checked a reference. "It's called the Underpass Trail. It leaves the Ortega Trail and passes under the freeway to where we will intersect with it. It then climbs rather steeply to the area where we were today."

McLeish was glancing at the map as he drove. "Won't our man use that trail himself? He'll want to leave the rifle somewhere on that knoll, right? And then get back down out of there as fast as possible."

Zack nodded. "Yes, he will more than likely make the same approach. It should be interesting."

"It will come down to who spots the other first," Eagle Feather said.

"That's it," Zack said. "Which is why you get to take point." He grinned at Eagle Feather.

"My father told me to beware of white men bearing gifts."

Barricades had been placed across the approach to the gap area in the northbound lanes and a patrol car with red lights guarded it. McLeish presented his credentials and they drove on.

"How do you think our perp will get through here?" McLeish asked.

No one had an answer.

They drove slowly into the tunnel. It was lighted so they turned off the headlights. The big surprise came after they exited the tunnel and saw a very bright light begin to appear around the bend. McLeish pulled over. "What the..."

Zack smacked his forehead. "Of course! We should have known Caltrans would be working tonight. It's critical for them to get this roadway open."

"That's how he'll do it," Eagle Feather said.

Both agents swung their heads to look at him.

"Who do what?" McLeish asked.

"I get it!" Zack said. "Eagle Feather's right! That's how our shooter will get in here to plant the rifle. He'll be dressed like a Caltrans worker."

"You mean in one of those yellow reflective bib things?"

"Exactly. He could park somewhere and saunter down the roadway with a shovel, have the rifle concealed in a bag of some sort."

"He might have planned this from the start," Eagle Feather said.

"How could he know if we didn't even think of it?" McLeish asked.

"He's had a lot longer to think about it," Zack said.

"He may have some connection with Caltrans and know how they work," Eagle Feather said.

They were still sitting there in the truck on the bench seat, staring out the windshield.

"So what now?" McLeish asked. "We can't walk out into those bright lights. If he's already there, it's game over."

"Maybe not," Zack said. "Where there's bright light, there's dark shadow. The big work job for Caltrans is the crater in the southbound lane. If they are working there, the lights could be directed away from the area we need to cross."

"Let's go see," Eagle Feather said and jumped out of the truck.

The two agents assembled their gear by the roadside. They put on dark camouflage jackets. Each shouldered a rifle and slung the tripod. Eagle Feather led off.

It worked out as Zack had predicted. The contrast between the very bright work lights in the southbound lanes and the unlighted northbound lane kept them in dark shadow. They hugged the far inside of the shoulder and stayed low to avoid sky-lining themselves against the lights. The noise of the earth moving machines covered any sounds they might have made.

Eagle Feather made a sign and then dropped out of sight. Zack followed him down a steep embankment. Here there was no light at all. He waited a moment for his night vision to come, felt an grip on his sleeve.

"There is a gully here. Stay close."

Zack heard McLeish slide down the rubble behind him. He reached back for him and relayed Eagle Feather's message. They gripped the back of one another's jackets, Eagle Feather leading, and slowly scrambled down the embankment to the bottom of the ravine. The highway bridge loomed next to them, echoing the sounds of the machines within its cavernous concrete hollow.

After clawing through brush and across loose rock they came to a path. Eagle Feather followed it away from the bridge and the highway. It took them through head-high reeds and under a large tree in deeper shadow. Zack had begun to see dim outlines as his vision adjusted. He was able to release his grip on Eagle Feather and felt McLeish let go of his jacket. The men paused under the tree.

"He could be anywhere around us now," Eagle Feather said into Zack's ear.

A steep slope was ahead of them. Above the lower reaches it was bright from the workmen's lights. He pulled Eagle Feather close, whispered, "What's up there?"

"That is the slope where he will leave the rifle."

Zack turned, reached for McLeish and whispered to him. "We are going up that slope. We need our rifles ready. Use your night scope. When we get to where you can sight the area of large rocks, drop out and set up to cover our advance." He felt an affirming squeeze from McLeish.

Beyond the tree more tall brush crowded the path, occasionally slapping back at Zack as Eagle Feather passed through. Where the path began to climb into the fire zone the undergrowth thinned. It angled into a gradual traverse as the grade steepened, then swung back the other way in a wide switchback.

When Zack realized he could see his own shadow he instinctively lowered his posture. They had passed out of the shadow of the low area and were now in silhouette against the work lights below. A meadow surrounded them, consumed by fire to bare stalks about boot high. As he glanced ahead looking for Eagle Feather, he saw a flash from above and heard the percussive report of a rifle. There was a plunk sound and a groan behind him.

Zack dropped and flattened out on the path. He called softly back to McLeish. "James, are you okay?"

There was no reply.

Zack kept his head down and crawled forward along the path several yards taking care not to disturb anything on either side. Stones protruded and there was loose gravel and ash and the path was steep. At one point he smelled sage. He groped around and found a cluster of roots just off the trail. He raised his head by increments behind the protective thickness of the burnt bush and peered through its branches, motionless, his eyes darting across the field above him. Light from the construction work below created a twilight around shadowy boulders and stunted trees. He saw no sign of Eagle Feather.

Zack thought the flame of the rifle had come from about eleven o'clock. He let his eyes continue to adjust to the low light and in a short time two large boulders took shape about two hundred yards above him in that direction. The boulders were maybe ten feet apart, Zack judged, but intense shadow hid the area between and beyond them. He waited and listened.

It was difficult to estimate the passing of time. Zack's neck ached from holding his head at this angle and his shoulders cried out for relief. There had been no other sound behind him. He guessed McLeish had been hit and immobilized by the rifleman, but he couldn't let his mind dwell on that now. There had been no sound, no sign of movement ahead on the path, no way to know where Eagle Feather had gone. There was no cover ahead so far as he could see. Not even Eagle Feather could advance without giving himself away.

A clink came to his ear, the tiniest sound of metal against stone. It seemed to come from the two boulders he watched. If it was the shooter and he had moved even the slightest bit, he would move again. Zack waited. His neck was in agony, his shoulder muscles screamed, but still he waited. His eyes lost focus, he blinked, looked away, looked back. Waited.

He saw it now, a place where shadow edged into light between the boulders, an imperfection in the stark outline, an anomaly. Without removing his eyes from it, Zack inched the rifle along the ground up the path in front of him, worked it around so the barrel faced toward his target, inch by inch. He willed the killer not to move while his hand found the stock and his finger found the trigger guard. He brought the scope up to his eye. The boulder surface leapt toward him remarkably clear in detail with blackened fungus patches and cracks. He inched the rifle along the boulder surface to its edge and into pointed grass stalks and along them and—there he was—a dark wide-brimmed hat, a splotchy white of forehead and now where the eye should be a cylindrical object and just below it the round opening of a rifle barrel pointed at him.

Zack fired.

CHAPTER TWENTY-SIX

Seconds after he pulled the trigger, Zack's left eye was blinded by the bright flash of the killers rifle. The two gunshots sounded as one. He heard the whine of a bullet pass his ear. He dropped to the ground.

He waited for his eye to recover. Following the muzzle flash, he thought he'd seen the figure drop away. But had he hit him? He must assume he'd missed. The killer might be very much alive and thinking these very same thoughts. Zack decided to give him something more to think about. He uttered a low groan, then immediately slithered flat on his stomach farther up the path.

Two shots rang out from the boulder area. Zack heard the thunk of the bullets in the dirt where he had been. He had two immediate thoughts—first, this rifleman was very good, and second, moving quickly away had been a good idea.

It was time for the waiting game again. Zack carefully rolled onto his back and lay flat with the rifle across his body like a horizontal sentinel, letting his cramped shoulders and sore neck relax. His hearing was restored and he listened. The usual night noises, the tree toads and slight rustlings and occasional muffled bird complaints were missing, only the basso continuo of the distant construction machinery came to him. Funny how those men could be so close, intent upon their jobs with no idea of the drama taking place on the hillside just above them.

How long had it been since that first shot? It might have been fifteen minutes, it might have been hours. Was McLeish still among the living? Zack harbored hope at first, but after this last exchange of fire his optimism faded. This shooter was very good. He would not have snapped a shot. He had watched their approach from his fortress up there among the boulders and made the deliberate decision to take out the last man of their group to contain them and then kill them off one at a time. Had it been Zack, he'd have concentrated on the lead man with his second shot. Eagle Feather must somehow have eluded the shooter.

Such tactics, such coolness under fire from the rifleman suggested military training. Zack had no doubt they were up against a professional.

Where was Eagle Feather? Could he have found a way off the path, some way to circle up behind? Remembering the terrain, Zack didn't think so. It would have been nearly impossible, there was no cover. Not even for Eagle Feather. Which meant his friend must be doing exactly what Zack was doing—waiting.

But waiting was to the advantage of the killer. If he had the skills, he could leave Bill's rifle where he was and sneak on up the slope and get away while Zack lay here doing nothing. The man had planned this tactic, had probably brought two rifles, his own and the one he'd taken from Bill. He'd leave Bill's rifle to incriminate him, take his own with him and disappear. Without any evidence to connect tonight's shooting to the pipeline business, it would be treated as a separate case and probably go unsolved.

Zack felt urgency. The killer might be escaping even now. Or he might be waiting, might expect Zack to understand the situation, make a rash move and offer himself as a target. Lose, lose.

But the killer had his own problem. He knew he had McLeish killed or wounded, he had Zack pinned down, maybe wounded, but he too must be questioning the whereabouts of Eagle Feather. If the killer tried to escape up the slope, he might crawl right into the Navajo's arms. In a sense, this was a stalemate between the shooter and Eagle Feather.

A shot rang out along with the ricochet sound of bullet off of stone. Was that Eagle Feather? But the Navajo did not have a rifle. In fact, as far as Zack knew his friend had no gun at all. Had the killer found Eagle Feather and fired at him? But the sound of the shot had come from below Zack, not above him. McLeish?

As if to answer his question there came rapid fire from the killer's position, a series of flashes directed toward McLeish's position down the hill. So James was still in the game! At least for now. Without thought, Zack rose and used the cover fire to dash a few yards up the trail, diving onto the path next to an earthen embankment in a puff of ash. He snuggled against the berm and felt the vibration of the series of bullets that sprayed into the earth above him.

He heard another report from McLeish's rifle, another ricochet. James was alive and able to fire. That was great news. The fact the killer had an automatic weapon was a less joyful thought. Yet the man's aim was not quite so good this time, a fact Zack attributed to the shooter's need to shift his rifle from one position to another quickly.

Zack's mind worked furiously. He knew the shooter was set up between the two boulders, which afforded him shelter from above and below. Twice now, McLeish's bullets had hit rock, which meant his angle was poor. Zack's angle was better, but now he had no cover other than the eight inch berm he snuggled against and the burnt grasses above it. He could do nothing here. He needed to move. But each foot up the path decreased his own angle of fire as the second boulder came into play. He thought he remembered that the trail angled up and slightly away from his current position. Somewhere, though, it turned directly upslope. All well and good, but it would take hours to crawl along the path on his stomach and another dash on foot in the face of this automatic weapon would be suicide.

He heard another shot from McLeish, heard the impact, a solid thunk. This bullet did not ricochet. James must have shot at the second boulder hoping to deflect a bullet inward toward the grassy area. A good thought, but the rock surface was too soft, the bullet had stuck. There was no return fire this time. The killer had made the tactical decision to concentrate on Zack as the more immediate threat of the two. If Zack rose now to dash up the path he'd be mowed down.

Another stalemate? What if the killer decided to move above the second boulder, out of McLeish's view but closer to Zack's position. Would he have a better angle of fire on Zack, trapped like a ground squirrel in his hole? Zack raised his eye an inch, then another but could see nothing above the earth furrow but black grass stalks. No, to see Zack the shooter would have to come much closer and in so doing become a target for McLeish.

Not yet a stalemate. Not while Zack could still move. Maybe up ahead along the path there was better cover. Pawn advances one square. He began to slither snail-like up the path. There was a sudden blast of automatic rifle fire. Zack froze, expecting a hail of bullets to thud into the earth around him. It didn't happen.

Zack could tell when a gun was fired in his direction. It makes an open, inclusive and very ominous sound. These shots were being fired in another direction entirely. Eagle Feather? But the Navajo should be somewhere up the slope from here. The killer was firing in the opposite direction. He must have turned his attention back to McLeish. And Zack realized something else. The man was no longer firing from the same position. While Zack had anticipated he would attempt to escape up the slope the man had changed strategies.

Of course. Eagle Feather. The wild card. Zack didn't know where he was, but neither did the killer. Rather than deal with both Zack and another invisible opponent somewhere above, this shifty strategist planned to storm the one man below by force of arms. McLeish was positioned well, protected by the slope for an assault on a pinned target above him. But he was very vulnerable to a skilled fighter with an automatic weapon moving down on him from cover to cover, keeping him pinned behind his tripod. At some point McLeish would have to break and run, and then he would be a dead man, an easy target against the glow of the construction lights. And that was if he could run. The killer knew McLeish had been hit. It was impossible to know how badly, but that possible immobility was another factor favoring the killer's new strategy.

The killer poured on the fire. Zack raised his head to view the flashes, saw the man was already well down the slope. Zack sent several bullets toward him to try to pin him down to no effect. There were too many unseen stumpy trees and boulders. Zack rose, dropped his rifle and bounded down the path. He had his Sig Saur in his hand now, racing to find a position for an effective shot, shooting to try to draw the killers attention, to slow him somehow. But the man's assault never waivered.

162

Zack was closing the distance, caught a root, slammed forward onto the ground, hit and rolled in a dusty ash cloud and rose again running, all in one motion, gun still in hand. But he had no chance. The figure of the killer closed on McLeish's position, the agent jumped up from concealment, tried to run, his left leg dragging. There was a single shot and McLeish went down.

Zack kept running, out of control down the path toward the killer, firing his pistol. The man turned, knelt and aimed his rifle. Zack snapped a shot, heard the click of an empty chamber. He threw his pistol at him in a long arc, his last hopeless gesture.

Movement caught his eye. A figure sprinting, leaping incredibly fast down the slope from the opposite side. As he saw the killer become aware, Zack jerked to one side and the bullet buzzed harmlessly by him. The man shifted to face the advancing figure but that second of delay had cost him, and Eagle Feather was on him. A knife blade flashed, the killer parried with his weapon, but the knife caught his hand and his rifle flew into the chaparral. He struck out with his other hand, a vicious stroke to the neck that backed Eagle Feather away, then he leg-whipped the Navajo off his feet and sent him rolling down the slope.

Now Zack was on the man, trying for a hold but it was like wrestling a mud-covered anaconda, the lithe strength and agility of the man left him no purchase. A sudden downward impact on Zack's nose stunned him, his grip weakened, and before he could recover the man was on his feet. Eagle Feather was scrambling back, crawling up to them, gathering his knees under him when the man delivered a vicious blow with his boot under the Navajo's chin. Eagle Feather went down.

The killer looked quickly for his weapon, gave it up and turned back up the trail at a half run. Zack was aware of his actions, but his vision was blurry, his body slow to respond to his will. Yet somehow he got unsteadily to his feet. He saw Eagle Feather stir but didn't wait, willing himself up the path moving faster as his body recovered. His vision was still blurred, he stumbled often, but somehow kept the dark path in front of him.

Zack did not expect he would catch the killer, didn't know what he could do even if he did. Those thoughts didn't enter his mind. There was just room for the will to keep moving. His fuzzy brain cleared bit by bit, his blood moving with his uphill run, and his deep breathing snapped his body back to a sensory memory of Quantico training. He looked up the path, beyond the switchback, toward the long row of big boulders and saw his quarry, a small black shadow moving steadily. A few hundred yards beyond those boulders, Zack knew, was the fire break and a trail intersection. Once the man reached it, he could turn in any direction and disappear. Zack could never catch him in time, yet he must.

Then, unaccountably, the man stopped, turned to face Zack, and waited.

CHAPTER TWENTY-SEVEN

Zack faltered, his numb brain slow to understand this new tactic from this fearsome enemy. The man's escape had been all but assured, yet now he stood waiting. Zack felt the danger, struggled to comprehend it, but kept running. Whatever was in store, he could not let the man escape.

The man stood where the path intersected with the row of large boulders. Zack was not yet close enough to distinguish his features, had seen only the camouflage clothing and camo face makeup during their struggle. Curious now, yet fearful, he slowed but kept approaching. Then he saw something else—the man was holding a rifle.

A rifle! Zack's fuzzy mind put it together now. It must be Bill Dench's rifle, the one the killer had left to incriminate him. Now he would use it to kill Zack. He knew Zack had no weapon. The man could have escaped but chose to remain to kill him, to complete his victory.

Zack was still jogging up the trail, close enough to see the whites of the man's eyes, the whiteness of his teeth against the black paint. Then the killer's eyes darted away from him. Zack glanced that way and saw Eagle Feather advancing steadily up through high grasses ten yards to his left, still below Zack but cutting the distance rapidly.

The killer watched, his eyes darted between them as if deciding who to shoot first. In that moment Zack recognized him.

"Halligon!"

"Agent Tolliver, you should take up a new line of work. You are too old and slow for this." He waved the tip of the rifle. "That's far enough. And tell your friend to stop where he is. He's close enough."

Zack said nothing.

Halligon kept his eyes on Zack while he shouted. "You! Stop right there. Another step and I will shoot your friend."

Zack returned Halligon's stare. Peripherally, he saw Eagle Feather's motion stop. Zack's mind flew to the rifle. He remembered the barn workshop and powder press, the cartridge cases on the bench top. Cartridges for four bullets! He was sure now Bill had been following Halligon's instructions, had loaded the rifle cartridge as he'd been told. One clean bullet to kill Bill, another clean bullet to puncture the gas pipeline, one incendiary bullet to blow it up, one incendiary bullet left chambered to incriminate Bill. That is all Halligon needed from Bill Dench when they rendezvoused on this hillside that night. Bill may have had more cartridges with him, but Halligon would not have taken them. He would have left them to further incriminate Dench.

"Which one of us will you shoot with your single bullet?"

Halligon looked startled, then smiled. "Very good, Tolliver. You are a card counter, I see. But don't worry, it will be you. I never really liked you from the first moment I saw you. As to your friend—"

Halligon's eye shifted to Eagle Feather and once again he looked startled.

Zack followed his gaze. There was no one there. Eagle Feather was gone.

Halligon's expression changed to anger. He shouted, "I told you not to move!" He looked at Zack, lifted his rifle. "Now you have killed your friend."

Ten yards of uphill slope separated Zack from the killer. There was no where to go, no way to evade a bullet, no way to rush the man. Zack felt a strange sense of calm fill his being. There was nothing to do, nothing to think, nothing but acceptance. He waited.

Halligon leveled the rifle at Zack. He did not fire. His eyes moved, drawn to something beyond Zack. His mouth gaped open.

Zack turned to look. He saw a large boulder, one of the many in that curious row across the hillside. It was rounded near the top with a bowl-shaped surface like all the others but there was a strange luminescence coming from the stone. Fog wrapped around the base of it like a blanket and as he watched the fog gathered and climbed. It took form and a pair of glowing red eyes appeared from within the swirling mist. Another boulder beyond it began to glow, wisps of this

166

same strange fog encircled and climbed it and a second pair of red eyes glared out of it.

Zack's head swung, watching in wonder as all the large boulders in the row along the hillside swirled with climbing mist. The fog-sheathed stones took form, the frightful red eyes looked toward them. The vague forms became human shapes, faces became defined, heads appeared on broad vaporous shoulders until one by one, silent as death, a battle line of ancient warriors stood upon each boulder, arms folded, their ominous and portentous gaze fixed upon the two humans cowering before them.

The men could only stare. The ancient eyes conveyed anger, denunciation, deep sorrow, a strange emptiness, fear, helplessness, so many other feelings for which Zack had no words, a cornucopia of emotions beyond his grasp and ability to assimilate as if all the terrible things ever done in the human world were now being expressed to him in this one moment. The message was from beyond this world, incomprehensible, unknowable and in its portent trivialized everything Zack had ever known or felt. The magnitude of the message reduced him to nothing. His mind swirled away. He was dust.

When Zack could see once again he was kneeling on the dirt path, head bowed, darkness surrounding him. Memory returned, he looked up and around. The boulders were only boulders, their dark shapes on the hillside vaguely illuminated by the lights from the work site. Halligon knelt where he had been standing, his head down as if overcome, his rifle on the ground forgotten.

Zack watched the man's head come up and their eyes met. Halligon slowly returned to awareness. Zack saw it in his eyes when memory was fully returned to him, saw the peaceful stillness of the man's features resume their former hard intent. Halligon reached for the rifle.

"I don't know how you did that, Tolliver, but it don't make no difference."

Zack was curiously unafraid as he watched Halligon grasp the weapon, raise it, check the chambered round, and aim it at Zack. The strange feeling of wonder from his experience filled him. Halligon might as well not have been there. Zack felt elevated beyond all that was happening. He had no recognition of imminent death, felt no desperate last minute urge to save himself. It somehow didn't matter.

He saw a confused look come over Halligon's face just as he prepared to pull the trigger, as if he couldn't understand why the man he was about to shoot was not afraid. In that moment a flash of shining metal appeared at Halligon's neck and John Halligon fell on his side. He twitched, made a gurgling attempt at words but expelled only blood.

Zack could not look away from the man's eyes, watched the same peaceful stillness return them. Then they went dull.

Eagle Feather strode into Zack's field of view and bending over the body removed his knife from Halligon's throat. He wiped the blood on his leather pants and sheathed the knife behind his back. He stood, legs apart, hands on hips, and stared down at Zack.

"What have you been smoking, White Man."

CHAPTER TWENTY-EIGHT

"I just don't understand," Irma Jean was saying. "What did this Halligon person have to do with my Bill, or with anything for that matter. He came here to kick us out, is all I know." None of the men gathered around the kitchen table had an answer ready for her. She took her coffee and followed Susan into the sitting room.

McLeish sat awkwardly on a kitchen chair loaded with extra cushions, his leg elevated on another. He'd risen from the dead a second time that night after his ballistic vest saved his life. The bullet had not penetrated his back, but had left a very sore and nasty bruise.

It was late morning at the Dench farm. The FBI agents had been up into the small hours the night before, working with the sheriff's office, giving statements. Supervisory Agent Janice Hooper had been on the phone with Zack several times. Today her team was looking into the background of John Halligon, a.k.a. Thomas Pence, a former Navy SEAL. The profile was coming together and it was very interesting.

It seemed that as a SEAL Halligon, then Pence, had been part of an operation in Colombia where he came into contact with coca growers and cocaine refiners. He left the SEALs after six years to take a private security job with an oil company based in Mexico. He did well, but apparently not well enough, for it was then he began to explore a unique path for importation of cocaine. It involved the use of oil pipelines. It took years to put it all together, it seemed, but eventually Pence, now Halligon, was heading a group that shipped cocaine from Colombia to the vicinity of the oil platforms off the coast of Santa Barbara County. From there, well-packaged "bullets" of cocaine were propelled through pipelines to land terminals where Halligon's inside man would shift them to the correct oil pipeline for the required destination. Within three to four years Halligon had his system operating at top efficiency. Money poured in and the entire team profited. Halligon oversaw the operation from supervisory jobs he took with pipeline companies, jobs easy to obtain with his credentials and the abundant money to grease the right palms. There was more research to be done, Janice admitted, but a picture was emerging.

"Halligon's turn of fortune seems to have begun with the rupture of the high pressure pipeline," Janice was saying. "That caused a nice mess along the shoreline. We suspect one or more of his cocaine bullets was in transit at the time. Maybe someone found something suspicious."

"When did Halligon obtain his job as security head on the pipeline?" Zack asked.

"Funny you should ask. His transfer came almost immediately after the leak. He put himself up for the job and they were happy to get him, I'm told."

Zack rubbed his chin, shifted the phone to his other hand. "So he wanted to keep an eye on the old pipeline, maybe to be first to know what might be found as sections are dug up?"

"That's my guess," Janice said. "Those so-called "bullets" must be pretty pricey. He'd know if one was still lodged in the pipeline's throat somewhere and would want to be on the scene when it is found."

"He must have had some idea where it would be. He would know it hadn't reached the next pump station, for instance, wouldn't he?"

Janice laughed. "For all we know, he could have a bug packaged with each bullet that sends out a signal so he'd know precisely where it is."

Zack breathed out. "I'll bet you're right."

After Janice rang off Zack discussed it with McLeish.

"Pretty amazing scheme," McLeish said.

Zack shook his head slowly. "But why the gas pipeline? Why blow that up?"

McLeish grinned. "Here's my guess. I bet Halligon knew just where his lost bullet was and it probably was somewhere just short of where he blew up the gas pipe." He pulled over a map from a stack on the kitchen table, opened it up. "See, look here. If the cocaine was lodged somewhere over this ridge, there'd be no way for him to get to it. It's in the state park, it's in a highly visible area, it's no longer under pressure—it's just sitting there underground in an oily pipe waiting to be dug up and replaced. Somebody is going to find it when they lay in the new pipe."

McLeish shifted a finger west on the map. "But just suppose something happened to induce the pipeline company to change the course of the new pipeline to somewhere over here, avoid the slopes of the gap entirely, avoid the Native American cultural site problem, all the park and environmental permit problems, all of it. They'd be dealing with private ownership. The ranch owners get a nice lease income for something that never comes above ground except for maybe a small pump station here and there. The line ends up west of the City of Buellton, where it's got to go anyway."

"Okay." Zack looked at McLeish, wondering where he was going with this.

"So what might induce a pipeline company to change the course of the new pipeline? Danger! Outcry by the public! The average Joe out there doesn't know the difference between a gas pipeline and an oil pipeline, or what kind of hazard each represents. All the public would care about is a pipeline blew up and killed a lot of people and endangered many more. So Halligon figures if he blows up the gas pipeline, causes enough damage, the oil pipeline company will be induced to change course in a way they'd like to do anyway!"

Zack saw it now. "So they change the course of the new oil pipeline and the old pipe lies there forgotten."

McLeish nodded. "Yep. Eventually the state gets the oil company to dig it out, maybe contracts a small crew to do it. And guess who would be in charge?"

"Halligon." Zack said. "Jesus, it just might have worked."

The rest of it was easy to work out. Doing due diligence in overseeing his pipeline cocaine delivery operation Halligon no doubt made it a point to familiarize himself with all the properties his merchandize must pass through in the pipeline. There were occasional stops and restarts of the oil flow caused by any number of unforeseen circumstances. He would have known that the possibility of a "bullet" becoming lodged in a pipe could occur anywhere, anytime. He would have discovered Bill Dench's farm early on and with a small amount of research have realized the man had no legal right to be living there. No doubt he tucked that knowledge away for future reference.

"Then the pipeline failure happens and strands some very expensive merchandise somewhere in the pipe," McLeish said.

"Right. That must have been a real blow. He had to find out where it was when everything stopped. His inside man at the Gaviota pump station would have signed off on it, so he knew it was somewhere between there and the next check-in location, probably the Sisquoc pump station."

"That's a lot of pipe."

Zack nodded. "Yeah, but I'm sure he's got a way to find it. I'll bet Janice was right. He probably inserted a transmitter in each package to keep tabs on its passage."

"Ballsy. Some random hunter with a radio might have picked up on that."

"Maybe. But unlikely. Let's not forget, this was a guy who lived on the edge because that's where he needed to be."

Zack gave McLeish a wan look and slowly climbed to his feet. "Speaking of living on the edge, or to be more precise beyond it, I guess it's time to inform Mrs. Dench about her husband's activities."

They gathered in the living room. Susan Colleen sat with Irma Jean on the couch and held her hand. James McLeish pulled a chair close. Zack sat forward on the edge of the second chair.

Irma Jean stared at Zack, a tear in the corner of her eye. "You are not going to tell me my husband was a criminal."

"No," Zack said. "I'm not. But I am going to tell you about the activities of a real criminal and how we believe your husband came to fall under his influence."

Irma Jean gave a slight sob and gripped Susan's hand tighter.

Zack breathed out, then began. "Your husband was a remarkable man. He had the rare capacity to look at old conventions in new ways. He was a pioneer, just as his forbears had been." Zack waved an arm. "What he has done here is remarkable. He has taken a completely primitive plot of land and made a self sustaining working ranch of it."

"But it wasn't his land to take." Irma Jean's tone was bitter.

Zack nodded. "Yes, that is the crux of the matter. He believed he had a right to the land. He believed it had been sold out from under his family, stolen, in his mind, a hundred years ago. It lay fallow. To him, it was the perfect place for his life experiment which in good faith and with love, he shared with you."

Irma Jean emitted another sob.

Zack continued. "His troubles began with the breach in the oil pipeline. At first, I believe Bill was outraged by the impact on the environment, the harm to the living creatures and the beauty of the landscape. But as time went on and the pipeline owner began negotiations for replacing the pipeline Bill began to see a threat to all he had built here. He knew the old pipeline route was nearby, the wide right of way planned for the new one would bring discovery and ruin. Meanwhile, there was another man equally concerned about the pipeline but for a very different reason. His name was Thomas Pence, A.K.A. John Halligon." Zack went on to tell Irma Jean what they had learned about Halligon.

McLeish joined in. "We believe Halligon devised a scheme to force the pipeline owners to choose an alternate route. He began by attempting to stir controversy among the parties opposed to the pipeline from the beginning, and there were many. However, he had little success. He did manage to provoke a small group of Chumash young people into a reaction. It was their ingenious laser light display of a woman dancing in flames that entertained late night travelers on the freeway through the gorge."

"We don't know how Halligon learned about the 1864 murder and burning of the Corliss couple," Zack said. "Maybe the Chumash youngsters knew the story. But there seems little doubt that Halligon fixed upon that bit of gruesome history as his theme to introduce fear of fire into a region already concerned about devastating fires. His next move upped the ante."

McLeish looked at Irma Jean. "We think this was when Halligon came to your husband and threatened him with exposure. We don't know what he planned, he may simply have wanted to force Bill to aid him in some way. But somehow in their conversations he must have learned of the death of your mother, and Bill's plans for her cremation."

"It must have come to him in a flash," Zack said. "Here was an opportunity to recreate the 1864 murder and burning with a real body. It would require a criminal investigation and the establishment of a crime scene right across the area where the new pipeline was to pass. It should bring a halt to further development in the gap area for some time.

"It must have taken some real arm twisting to get Bill to agree. But some part of your husband must have seen it as visual recompense for the wrong done his family so long ago. In any case, when cremating your mother in his retort furnace he added several wine barrel hoops, kept her ashes for your memorial but permitted Halligon to remove some bone with fused hoops for the fake crime scene."

Irma Jean was beyond speech. Susan put a strong arm around her shoulders and held her.

Zack ploughed on. "But Halligon had much more in mind, and he wasn't about to let your husband off the hook. Bill was in deep now, and both men knew it. Halligon's next move was meant to divert suspicion from himself and onto your husband. He organized to be at the crime scene when Agent McLeish and I arrived that first day. Bill was positioned across the valley with his rifle and at a prearranged signal sent a bullet close to Halligon. As we all know, Bill was an experienced woodsman and an excellent shot and accomplished this easily. It worked to perfection." Zack glanced at McLeish, who nodded.

McLeish put up open palms. "Not once did we suspect Halligon of wrong doing. We can only surmise what Halligon promised Bill next, probably that it would be the last thing he'd require of him. Whatever it was, he convinced him. He had Bill load the cartridges for his rifle specifically with two incendiary bullets and two non-incendiary bullets in a specific order. No doubt he assured Bill that if he delivered the rifle loaded in that manner to him in a specific place at a specific time their business would be at an end and Bill would be free to go his own way." McLeish shrugged. "Whether Bill actually believed him is a matter for conjecture, but after all, what choice did he have? He could only hope it was true."

Zack's voice was grim. "It was a plan for murder start to finish. Halligon never intended for Bill to walk away from the scene of the gas explosion. He picked his location carefully, a place he could murder Bill with his own rifle, then shoot the gas pipeline with the non-incendiary bullet and let the gas flow enough so that an incendiary bullet would immediately ignite it. Then he'd leave the rifle near Bill's body with the second incendiary bullet chambered as incriminating evidence and escape before the flames consumed the hillside where he stood."

Zack glanced at McLeish. "We think Bill suspected something as soon as he handed his rifle over. He probably turned and ran downhill. Halligon shot him, but by then Bill had come too close to the potential explosion for Halligon's own safety. He must then have realized he'd have to keep the rifle and see what developed. So he went ahead and shot the pipeline with the penetrating bullet, climbed a safe distance up the hillside as the gas accumulated, and then ignited it."

"The explosion was probably greater than Halligon expected," McLeish said. "He couldn't get back to Bill's body nor could he throw the rifle far enough, so he took it with him. Sooner or later, he had to get rid of it but—not just anywhere."

"That's how we knew he'd be back last night," Zack said.

CHAPTER TWENTY-NINE

The invitation to dine at the Willows in the Chumash Casino came as a surprise to Zack, particularly since the host's name on the fancy invitation was Eagle Feather. Zack realized his friend knew people there but he also knew the Willows was the casino's most expensive restaurant, a four diamond establishment.

Zack was packing up. The case was solved. James McLeish would handle the reports on the local front, including all media interviews. There would be many. Zack's report would go to Janice and she'd decide where it would go from there, particularly concerning the ancient Indian warrior specters. He loaded up the Cherokee, paid his bill, and drove to the casino. After this posh dinner, he'd return the Jeep to the base and take the flight to Flagstaff that Spud had arranged. As he drove through Solvang, observing the Danish flags, thatched roofs and faux storks he had mixed feelings. It had been a difficult case, there had been unfortunate loss of life and property, and a widow left with slim prospects. On the other hand, they'd solved it, caught the killer and a major trafficker, and done some good as well. But weren't the difficult cases always like this? His real pleasure came from knowing he was about to go home to be with Libby and Bernie and put his feet up and enjoy his family. And write his report.

He parked the Cherokee in the casino garage and took the elevator to the gaming floor where he received directions to the Willows. To his surprise, he was led to a table set for six. Three faces looked up at his approach.

McLeish stood, his hands on the shoulders of an attractive middle-aged blonde woman. "Zack, I'd like you to meet my wife, Maybelline."

Zack reached out a hand and Maybelline took it, blue eyes twinkling. "So you're the reason I haven't seen my husband for five days."

"Only partly," Zack said with a grin. "Only partly."

He looked across the table as he sat. "Well, hello, Spud."

"Hello yourself. Are you the reason I'm here?"

"I am not." Zack looked at McLeish, eyebrows raised.

"Don't look at me. I got an invitation from Eagle Feather stating time and place and please bring the missis."

Zack shook his head in wonder. "Right when you think you know the guy."

Spud's eyes glanced beyond Zack. Zack looked over his shoulder and saw Eagle Feather approaching. He wore his best leather vest with bead necklaces, shiny leather pants and his hat was brushed and shiny. Only the solitary limp feather was unchanged. On his arm was a stunningly beautiful woman.

By now the entire party was standing. They gave an impulsive ovation.

To Zack's surprise, the woman came directly to him and kissed him on his cheek. "Hello, Zack, it's good to see you again."

Zack could only stare. "Shana, is it really you?"

She smiled. He had forgotten how beautiful her brown eyes were, flecked with gold as if bejeweled.

Zack was stunned. "How did you...when did you...?"

"You had better sit down, White Man, before you fall down," Eagle Feather said.

Zack dropped into his chair.

"Please sit, everyone," Eagle Feather said. "We are making a scene."

After everyone was seated, all eyes on Shana, Eagle Feather said, "Allow me to introduce Miss Shana Bows, Tribal Council Chair Person of the Southern Paiute Band of Indians. And my date."

"Please call me Shana," she said with a mischievous smile. "Not his date."

Eagle Feather gave her a glance, at once unsmiling yet somehow infused with fondness. "She is a person to be reckoned with in her own right."

Zack was still putting it together in his mind. He stared at Eagle Feather. "You told me you were staying here because you had a friend in high places." He pointed a finger up to the sky and the tower rooms. "You meant your friend was in the high places."

Shana blushed an attractive shade of pink.

"Now you are just plain being rude, White Man. I can dress you down but I cannot take you out."

Shana reached out a hand to cover Zack's. "When I learned you had a case in this area and needed Eagle Feather, I called an old friend who made our arrangements. Tribal leader Kane and I have worked closely together to promote Native American welfare. We took the opportunity to meet and plan while Eagle Feather was off wandering in the woods."

McLeish broke in, spreading his arms wide. "And this?"

Shana smiled. "This is a thank you from my friend for resolving the crime in Las Cruces. He is particularly grateful you were able to show the Chumash had no part in it. And"—she patted Zack's hand— "for keeping the shenanigans of the young Chumash students quiet."

A waiter arrived with six tall glasses of champagne.

Zack stood first. "A toast to Eagle Feather, the most remarkable, loyal, and critical friend and mentor anyone could desire."

A chorus of "Here! Here!" rose from the group and glasses touched.

Eagle Feather stared straight ahead as Shana smiled proudly.

McLeish stood next. "I haven't known Agent Tolliver as long as you all have, but from what I've heard, the fact that I'm having trouble standing right now can be expected when working with this man, a truly dedicated, relentless champion of truth and freedom."

Eagle Feather's "Here! Here!" was the loudest of all.

The toasts went on for probably longer than appropriate until finally the soup arrived and everyone focused on their food.

It was Spud who said, "I can't help thinking about poor Mrs. Dench."

Zack nodded. "She has nothing now—no husband, no home, no job."

"Whoa, not so fast," McLeish said. "I've just learned something interesting from the County Supervisor. It appears Bill Dench was even more clever than we thought. Seems he's been paying taxes every year on that property he didn't own."

Spud's head jerked up. "What? Why would he do that?"

"It seems in California there is something called an Adverse Possession Law. You can stake a hostile claim on a property and actually come into possession of it. But you have to honestly believe you are the rightful owner through an incorrect deed or incorrect sale of the property."

"That happened, didn't it?" Zack said. "Or at least Dench believed it did after the Corliss murders and the various court cases that followed."

McLeish nodded. "That's right."

"So if you—"

"If you believe you are the rightful owner, you occupy the land, you are aware you are trespassing, you live on the land as if it is your own publicly and in the open, and you continuously use the land for five years you can take possession."

"How did—"

McLeish favored the group with an enigmatic smile. "It seems the police matron Susan Colleen also happens to be a pretty good law student. Once she learned from Irma Jean that Bill had been paying taxes, she figured out what he'd been up to and filed for ownership on Irma Jean's behalf."

'But wait," Zack said. "I thought that area was owned by the state."

"It is, well, was," McLeish said. "You see, the wrongful sale Bill claimed on behalf of his antecedents preceded the sale to the state and therefore supersedes it. If this filing is accepted, the state never actually had ownership of that land."

"Well, my goodness," Maybelline said. "What a turn around." She looked at her husband. "So that's why you were on the phone all afternoon."

He smiled sheepishly.

The desserts dishes were taken away and coffee served. Spud caught Zack's eye. "You have a plane to catch if you want to get to Flagstaff tonight."

"Oh, I do, I do." He glanced at his watch and rose from his seat.

Zack's leaving signaled a general dispersal, with farewells and promises to stay in touch. Shana deposited a warm kiss on Zack's cheek before she disappeared upstairs. Eagle Feather walked with him to the parking garage.

"Your first case went well."

"You rascal. How long have you and Shana been dating?"

"You ask many questions, White Man."

Zack laughed and gave his friend a fond look. "And you share very few answers. Such as where you disappeared to when those ghost warriors rose from the rocks. And why they didn't seem to effect you as they did me."

Eagle Feather looked at Zack with lifted eyebrows. "The answer to that is simple. It is because you are still a white man, White Man."

Thank you for purchasing LAS CRUCES. I know you could have picked any number of books to read, but you picked this book and for that I am grateful.

I hope you found it enjoyable. If so, please consider posting a review on Amazon.com. Your feedback and support will help this author improve his writing craft for future projects and make this book even better. Please also consider sharing this title with your friends and family by posting to Facebook and Twitter. I'd also enjoy hearing from you personally at lawsongamble@rlawsongamble.com.

Happy Reading!

AUTHOR'S NOTE

Fiction is fiction and fact is fact. Occasionally the latter transcends the former in terms of irony, strangeness, and the power to effect the reader's emotions. The story presented in Chapter Three about the sad fate of Trecia and George Corliss is fact. The story spun from it is fiction.

The trails of Gaviota State Park, the gas pipelines, the nearby oil pipelines, the U.S. 101 Freeway through the gap all exist. The boulders on the slope opposite the Ortega Trail from whence rose the Ancient Warriors are there to be found by the imaginative. The archeology of early Native Americans in and through the Gap exists. The Las Cruces Adobe and other relics of early European settlement may still be found.

The new pipeline will be constructed, the culture built upon the oil industry will fight to live on and will leave its mark for good and ill before it finally succumbs, as have all cultures built upon a single industry in human history.

Our reality springs from our turbulent history and our future is set by our present reality. It was always thus and so it shall always be.

ABOUT THE AUTHOR

R Lawson Gamble enjoys the Southwest, great stories, Indian lore and culture, and scary paranormal possibilities, all of which find their way into the *ZACK TOLLIVER, FBI* series of novels.
The author lives in Los Alamos, California among the beautiful Central Coast Golden Hills. He enjoys hearing from fans at LawsonGamble@RLawsonGamble.com

Made in the USA
Monee, IL
26 December 2024

75479396R00111